DIAMOND

Mage

OTHER BOOKS BY DOROTHY DREYER

Phoenix Descending

Paragon Rising

Cauldron of Ash

Christmas in Silverwood

THE EMPIRE OF THE LOTUS SERIES

Crimson Mage

Copper Mage

Golden Mage

Emerald Mage

Sapphire Mage

Amethyst Mage

Diamond Mage

DIAMOND

Mage

EMPIRE OF THE LOTUS

BOOK SEVEN

DOROTHY DREYER

Diamond Mage
Empire of the Lotus Book Seven

Copyright © 2021 Dorothy Dreyer
Edited by Amy McNulty
Cover design by Sora Sanders

Paperback ISBN: 978-1-948661-47-8

Published March 2021 by Snowy Wings Publishing
PO Box 1035, Turner, OR 97392

For my brilliant ARC team

who keeps me motivated

Everything has changed. And it could mean the end of the world.

The comet has arrived. The elite mages, once primed to hold their ground, now find themselves in a panic. They've been separated, and the upper hand they once called their own has been stolen from right under their noses.

The Pishacha are ready to release Kashmeru from his tomb, to destroy the Lotus empress, and follow their dark god into the new era. To stop them, the elite mages must give up the very thing they've been fighting for—and hope it's enough to win the war.

Whether we fall by ambition,

blood, or lust,

like diamonds we are cut

with our own dust.

— John Webster

The legend goes …

The ancient deity Kashmeru knew only one true love—the Lotus empress Lakshmi, who in his eyes possessed all beauty and grace the universe could hold. Their hearts called to one another, a hold so strong that neither one could deny the bond. But Lakshmi knew that Kashmeru's spirit was not pure, for an evil dwelled within his soul, a wickedness so corrupt that it could destroy the universe.

And when she denied him her love, destroying the universe was the very thing he vowed to do.

Throughout the centuries, their reincarnations were drawn to one another, but the outcome was always the same: Lakshmi would never give Kashmeru her heart.

To put an end to his constant chase, the Empire of the Lotus defeated Kashmeru and sealed him in a tomb using mage powers, where he would remain trapped …

… until the Council of the Seven could secure the blood of the Lotus empress to set him free.

THE SEVEN HOUSES OF MAGES

Crimson: earth, stability, survival, security.

Copper: water, ice, pleasure, guilt.

Golden: fire, willpower, shame.

Emerald: air, wind, heart, love, grief.

Sapphire: throat, sound, truth, lies.

Amethyst: vision, sight, illusions, secrets.

Diamond: spirituality, emotion, virtue, integrity.

One

Darshana tensed her muscles, a rush of adrenaline coursing through her as her pulse hammered in her throat. She gritted her teeth, pacing the main room of the house, as her heightened senses set off alarms in her head.

Danger.

Her mind raced, trying to make sense of the overload of images ripping through her head. Her breaths came hard and fast as she tried to see and hear everything at once, but the visions were muddled, unclear, and she found it hard to put them in the right order.

"Darshana?"

She flinched, as if the voice knocked her from her thoughts. She turned to the man, her mind slowly coming to the realization that it was Mr. Kitaro speaking to her. He tilted his head, his salt and pepper hair, which was usually slicked back, sat unusually disheveled.

Wringing her hands, she gave an apologetic bow to Mr. Kitaro. "I'm sorry."

"What's wrong?" he asked, studying her. "Has something happened?"

"I believe so." She solemnly shook her head. Her fingers reached for her long braid which lay over her shoulder and worried the white strands. "But I can't make heads nor tails of it."

Mr. Kitaro glanced over his shoulder, seemingly unsure of what to do.

"Check on the elites." The words barely left Darshana's lips before she darted toward the bedrooms.

Mr. Kitaro followed, and they each knocked on and opened the doors down the long hallway, calling out the names of the others.

Loni wrinkled her brow as she came to the door and met the anxiousness in Darshana's eyes.

"What's wrong?" Salina's golden-flecked eyes were wide with concern as she stepped out into the hall.

Jae and Shiro soon joined her, obvious confusion on their faces.

"Did something happen?" Jae asked. "Is it Naree?"

Darshana slowly turned to them, her gaze intense as she pressed her fingertips together. "Where are the others? Mayhara, Yuki, Penny, and Karina?"

The others exchanged glances.

"They're not in the house? But it's dark outside." Salina marched toward the kitchen.

Loni furrowed her brow and darted toward the front door, leaving it open as she ran outside.

Jae whipped out his Linq. Shiro did the same. Darshana pressed her fingertips to her lips and forced herself to keep her breathing steady.

"Mayhara's Linq goes straight to voicemail," Jae said after pressing his Linq to his ear for a moment.

"Yuki's as well," Shiro added.

Salina returned from the main room, chewing on a nail. "Are they out training? Not that we're panicking for no reason?"

"This late at night?" Shiro asked.

"Maybe they wanted to test their powers again." Salina shook her head, as if she knew her theory was unlikely.

Loni stomped back into the house. "I can't see them anywhere."

Darshana's hands were clammy, the hairs lifting from the nape of her neck. "No. They're in trouble. I can feel it."

"But where are they?" Mr. Kitaro asked. "The property is big, but they can't have gotten far."

"Maybe you're forgetting," Loni said to him, "that the Pishacha can travel in clouds of smoke. They could have easily popped in for an attack and left again."

"We'll need to search the property, then," Mr. Kitaro rubbed a hand across his jaw. "If they're injured and lying out in one of the fields…"

"No." Darshana held her palms against her cheeks, her eyes narrowing. "No, they're not on the property. They're far. And I can't be sure, but I feel as if their energy is dispersed."

"Dispersed?" Jae asked.

"Like they're not together?" Shiro asked.

"You think they were kidnapped?" Salina asked.

Loni squared her jaw. "It wouldn't be the first time."

"What do we do?" Salina asked.

"Well, whatever we decide—" Mr. Kitaro's glance darted between them all. "—we can't stay here."

Salina blinked rapidly. "What?"

Darshana let out a sigh, her brows drawn together. "We have to come to terms with the fact that we've most likely been compromised. If the Pishacha have indeed kidnapped the others—or worse—then we cannot remain here as sitting targets for another attack."

Mr. Kitaro suddenly flinched, as if something troubling occurred to him. He turned on his heel and bolted into his office. Darshana exchanged looks with Jae. In a matter of seconds, Mr. Kitaro reappeared in the hall.

"It's gone," he said, color draining from his face.

"What is?" Salina asked.

"The dagger I was in charge of." He swallowed hard. "It's been stolen."

Darshana worried the knuckles of one hand. "I have a

feeling it's not the only one missing."

Loni pressed her fingertips to her temples and let out a curse.

"We can check." Salina's hands clenched into fists. "Take inventory to see where we stand. But then what? What do we do? Where do we go?"

Darshana inhaled deeply, pushing down her panic. "We need to try to locate the others. To figure out how to rescue them. I can feel they need us. But in the meantime, we'll move on towards the Lotus temple. It's earlier than originally planned, I know. But it's the next logical step."

"And then what?" Shiro asked.

"And then we hope the gods have blessed us with a miracle to win this war."

Two

Karina's pulse was like a jackhammer, pounding with the force of a thousand cannons and threatening to break her into pieces. She found it hard to breathe, and the only thing that kept her from completely losing it was the determination to save Penny from Bhutano's control.

Her eyes were still trying to adjust from the blast of black smoke that had filled her vision when the enemy had grabbed her and teleported with her from Mr. Kitaro's property. She must have blacked out when it had happened because she couldn't remember anything up until this moment. She replayed the scene in her head, trying to figure out what exactly might have happened to Mayhara and Yuki. She swallowed back the lump in her throat, her muscles tensing as she tried to slow her heartbeat.

There had been six of them in the woods. Karina had walked there with Mayhara and Yuki to discuss their suspicions about Penny. And Penny—whom they now knew was being possessed and controlled by Kashmeru's spirit messenger, Bhutano—had shown up with a Pishacha soldier and one of the dark mages.

Their sudden appearance had resulted in a standoff for the scroll Karina had carried. But Karina had tossed the scroll to Yuki and Mayhara, along with a spell that would transport them somewhere safe. The problem was Karina wasn't sure where that safe place might have been.

This concern was coupled with the fact that Yuki had fired diamond bullets with her mage powers in order to stop Avi—the dark mage—from crushing their bones with his magic. One of the stray bullets had hit Penny. And even through it had been Bhutano controlling Penny's body, Karina knew the real Penny inside would surely die along with Bhutano if Karina didn't use her magic to help them.

To top things off, Avi, who had also been wounded by Yuki's bullets, had somehow gotten sucked into Karina's spell and disappeared with them. Although Karina suspected Yuki's diamond magic might have mixed with her, and she had no idea what the consequences of such a magical combination could be.

Lastly, Karina felt an urgency to get word to the other mages and Darshana. They were all in danger, and the enemy had stolen all the arcane daggers from them. With the daggers and the grimoire in their hands, they had all the ingredients they needed to release Kashmeru from his tomb, which meant the certain end of the world.

But Karina was helpless to do anything because Bhutano and Pishacha had abducted her, and she had no idea how she was going to turn the tables on the enemy.

As she blinked away the last of the smoky dust from her eyes, she glanced around and studied her location. It wasn't what she'd expected. Judging from the view out the window, she was in an extravagant apartment in some high-rise. Probably the penthouse. She wasn't sure what city they were in, though. Not far from where she sat, the most beautiful young woman she'd ever seen hovered over Penny and inspected her injury.

Naree. The empress. The reincarnated goddess they called "the Lotus."

She could tell just by looking at her that she was royalty. Her thick, long, dark hair looked as if it were spun silk. Her brown eyes practically glittered like jewels. There was an aura around her that was mesmerizing. Karina had never seen such perfect, glowing skin before.

Karina was on the floor, her back against the wall, and her legs trapped in warped metal clamped around her thighs. When she lifted her gaze, she spotted a dark mage watching her from a chair in the living room. Though he was indoors, he wore a long, dark gray cloak over a loose, white shirt. His hair was buzzed short on the sides, but the longer portion from the top was pulled back into a ponytail. She could just make out the top of a tattoo decorating his neck. He smirked when his eyes traveled down to the warped metal. The look of pride on his face told Karina that he was the one who had manipulated the contraption.

"She's awake," the dark mage called out.

Naree looked up and stood straighter.

Bhutano sat on a barstool, his jaw clenched and hands covering the bloody wound. "Thank you, Rikuto." The purple-flecked brown eyes that were really Penny's drifted from the dark mage over to Karina.

Naree waltzed over to her as if she had all the time in the world. "So you're the witch."

Karina breathed deeply through her nose, her eyes trained on the beautiful empress.

Naree lifted her chin and glanced back at Bhutano, who slowly made his way over to join her.

"She doesn't look like the most powerful witch in New United Asia," Naree said.

Karina had never been one to fuss about her appearance, but the way Naree was looking at her made her want to tame her wild hair and hide the tears in her clothes.

"But she is," Bhutano said, wincing. "I don't know what spell she used, but she made two of the elite disappear, and Avi along with them. Who knows what alternate realm she might have spelled them to?"

"Hmm." Naree placed her hands on her hips. "That does pose a problem."

A figure lurking near the door stepped into the room. The woman appeared to be in her mid-to-late thirties. A small touch of wrinkles marked the space between her dark brows. Her dark hair lay flat, almost oily in texture, with a few gray strands tucked behind her ears. The most prominent feature on her face was her nose, below which hung a round, silver piercing. "She absorbed her grandmother's powers, but she still has no control over them."

Karina narrowed her eyes at the woman. Why would she say such things? This woman didn't even know her.

The woman traipsed over to her, studying her with judgement in her eyes. The closer she got, the more Karina was filled with the need to protect herself.

"You don't need her," the woman said. "My skills as a witch are exemplary. And I'm in control of them." She reached for Karina's hair. "My powers are far more—"

The second her fingers curled around a lock of Karina's hair, the woman's eyes widened and her face went pale. She quickly retracted her hand as if she'd been stung, pulling it to her chest and covering it with her other hand, gaping at Karina.

"How did you do that?" the woman—the witch, Karina now comprehended—asked in shock.

"Her hair." Bhutano shifted closer, clutching at his wound. "The strands Tien Thi touched…"

Karina threw him a questioning look. She grabbed at her hair and pulled it forward so she could see it. The small section of hair in her hand had strands that had gone from messy, dark brown to silky, reddish gold. Her jaw dropped for a second. This was what her hair had looked like when she'd been a child. The conversation she had had with her grandmother when Karina had been young came to mind, where Amalia had told her that witches born with this color hair were special and fated for particular destinies. Karina quickly snapped her mouth shut and stared at her captors.

"I told you she was powerful," Bhutano said with a strained voice.

The bandage covering his wound was already soaked with fresh blood, and Karina worried Penny was running out of time.

Tien Thi pursed her lips and narrowed her eyes, her

hand still cupped against her chest. "She had no control of it, though. Her magic is too wild."

Naree raised a hand. "That's enough, Tien Thi. I will decide if she has value or not."

Karina's mind was racing, trying to figure out how to use her status to her advantage. "I can control it." She kept her chin up and erased any evidence of doubt from her features. "And I have a proposition."

Bhutano and Rikuto exchanged a wary glance, but Naree kept her eyes on Karina.

"What is your proposal?" Naree asked.

"We both want something here," Karina began. "We both have something to negotiate with."

Tien Thi scoffed. "We're not here to negotiate with you, you imbecile."

Naree squared her jaw. "I said *that's enough*, Tien Thi. Let her speak."

Karina's gaze darted between them. "You need a powerful witch to unlock Kashmeru's tomb. I'll agree to be that witch, perform the spell for you."

Tien Thi appeared as if she were about to retort, but Naree flashed her a warning glare.

"Continue," Naree said to Karina. "What is it you

want in exchange? I'll admit Tien Thi is annoying, but she has a point: You're not exactly in a position to negotiate."

"You know I can do it," Karina insisted. "You've only got one shot at getting that tomb open, and I'm your best bet. I've absorbed my grandmother's powers, and I was marked a special witch as a child." She swallowed hard. "I hate to admit it, but all signs turn to one undeniable fact: I was born to do this."

Naree scrutinized her face. "And what is it you want in return?"

"Release Penny."

At first, Naree simply gaped at her.

Karina continued. "Let me heal her wound and then set her free from Bhutano's possession."

"That's an awfully bold demand," Naree stated. "You expect me to simply release an enemy from my control?"

"It won't matter in the long run, if you think about it." Karina winced as she tried to shift within her metal trap. "The comet is just a couple of days away. You have all the daggers. There's nothing to stop us from releasing Kashmeru."

"Then why would it make a difference if we released your friend when she's doomed anyway?"

"It makes a difference to me." Karina shook her head. "I'll know I did everything I could… for her. To end her suffering. And anyway, if you deny me, I'll refuse to help you."

Naree looked her over. "I believe she means it."

"Your Highness?" Bhutano appeared skeptical.

Naree turned to him. "You have many of Kashmeru's followers available, ready to serve as a vessel for your spirit. And as for the amethyst mage, I can sweep her mind."

Karina gasped. "What? No!"

Naree's head swiveled back to face Karina. "Those are my terms. You may heal your friend, and we will release her. But her mind will be erased. Take it or leave it."

Karina could hardly breathe. She looked into Penny's eyes, hoping she could make her understand that she was doing this for her. The lump in her throat almost choked her as she swallowed it back.

Naree crossed her arms, one brow raised as she waited for Karina's answer.

"Very well," Karina finally said.

Naree smirked and uncrossed her arms. "Rikuto, you may remove her binds."

Rikuto kept a straight face as he approached Karina.

DIAMOND *Mage*

He held out his palms toward her, and a dusty black mist emerged, traveling from his hands to the warped metal. Karina felt the pressure ease on her thighs as the metal loosened and eventually unraveled. When she was free enough, she hurried to her feet but kept close to the wall, just in case.

"This is absurd," Tien Thi said, her hands balled into fists. "What of me? Do you just expect me to stand by and allow this to happen?"

Naree frowned at the witch. "No. That's not exactly what I had in mind."

"Then what?" Tien Thi stared at her expectantly.

Naree eyed Rikuto. "It looks like we no longer have the need for the lesser witch."

Tien Thi gasped. Rikuto gave Naree a nod.

Faster than Karina could follow, Rikuto shifted his wrist, and a jagged sliver of the metal ripped itself from the piece that once bound her legs. It flew swiftly toward Tien Thi and sliced across her neck.

Karina slapped a hand over her mouth as blood gushed and spurted from the witch's throat and she dropped, wide-eyed, to the floor.

Three

Yuki felt sick to her stomach. Her head spun, and her vision blurred. She wasn't even sure she was standing upright. Stretching out her hand to find her bearings, she felt someone's fingers wrap around hers.

"Mayhara?" Yuki blinked and squinted, hoping the

hazy fog that obscured her vision would clear.

"I'm here," Mayhara answered. "Wherever *here* is."

Bit by bit, Mayhara's face came into view. There was fear and confusion in her big, brown eyes, and small wrinkles formed on the forehead of her heart-shaped face.

Yuki took in deep breaths, trying to calm the bubbling churn of her stomach. She glanced around, taking in their surroundings in an attempt to figure out where they might be.

"What happened?" Mayhara asked, raking the fingers of one hand through her dark brunette waves. In her other hand was Karina's small satchel. "How did we get here?"

Yuki wiped her shaking hands on her jeans and shook her head. "I'm not sure. I used my powers to divert our plane momentarily—"

"Wait? What? I... I don't know what that means."

"Okay. Sorry. It's a power diamond mages can develop. We're connected to spirituality and the spirit realm."

Mayhara's eyes widened slightly. "Are you saying we're in the spirit realm?"

Yuki glanced over her shoulders, unsure of how to answer. "I didn't mean for us to land here. I didn't even know it was possible. I was just trying to shift our place in our plane of existence so Avi couldn't get to us." She eyes the small bag Mayhara clutched to her chest. It contained the scroll that held the spell that could destroy Kashmeru. "I couldn't let him get his hands on the scroll."

Mayhara ran her hand over the satchel as she nodded. "Right. Okay. So then, how did we end up here?"

Yuki replayed the scene in her head. She remembered Karina shouting words she didn't understand. And she remembered feeling a wave of energy wash over her.

"Karina cast a spell. I can't be sure what the spell was, but I think it somehow melded with my powers and… sent us here."

"Wherever *here* is." Mayhara slowly turned her head, her eyes scanning the area. "If we landed here, I wonder what happened to Karina."

"And Penny. I mean, I know it was Bhutano controlling her, but I still believe Penny was in there somewhere. I hope they're all right."

Yuki pushed her auburn hair out of her face and surveyed their surroundings. Everything around them seemed slightly out of focus, as if some kind of filter was on that caused a slight glow. At their feet, a low fog traveled, touching upon everything as it floated along. The air was cool, almost chilly, and smelled as if there might be a bonfire nearby. The buzzing of insects seemed higher-pitched than normal. But the most unusual thing was a shimmering, multicolored haze that danced slowly around the sun. The haze changed hues as it moved, reminding Yuki of the *aurora borealis*, the northern lights that were predominantly seen in high-latitude regions. Also marking the sky was a dark streak. It was like the negative image of the comet, and Yuki wondered if the blackness of it was symbolic of impending doom.

"So now the question is," Mayhara began, worrying the strap of the satchel, "how do we get out of here?"

Yuki tried to steady her breaths. She could feel Mayhara's anxiety, and it matched her own. At least she *thought* it was Mayhara's anxiety. She briefly wondered if her own emotions were so strong, she couldn't feel past them. But she had to try to keep them both calm so they could use their heads and figure out their next move. It wouldn't do either of them any good if she gave in to her panic.

A snapping of a nearby branch made them both jump. They huddled together, both raising a hand with their palms facing outward, preparing for whoever or whatever might be approaching. This realm was unfamiliar, and Yuki didn't know what to expect.

Movement caught her eye. Yuki's breath caught in her throat when she spotted Avi—the dark mage who'd tried to kill them just moments before—stumbling out from behind a far-off tree.

"No. How did—?" Mayhara couldn't even finish her question.

"He must have got caught in the magic mashup or something." Yuki kept her voice low, but it was too late. Avi had already noticed them.

Wild brunette hair framed his boyish face, but instead of his usual pompous and arrogant expression, his features here riddled with a combination of fury and pain. He bit on his thick bottom lip as he hobbled toward them. Yuki could see blood seeping through his clothes at his waist and shoulder.

A part of her felt bad for having injured him. She had cared for him once, when they'd first become involved with each other. He had been charming and funny, and she'd never been looked at by anyone else the way Avi had looked at her.

But everything had changed when she'd found out what side he was on. She felt like the whole thing had been a lie. And now, he seemed hellbent on killing her. On killing her and Mayhara both.

Avi gritted his teeth and lifted a blood-soaked hand. Yuki grabbed Mayhara's arm and began to pull her back, away from Avi. But when he frowned and examined his hand, Yuki took a relieved breath. There had been no black tendrils, no cloud of black smoke, and more importantly, no pain. It appeared Avi's bone-crushing dark magic had failed.

"His powers," Yuki whispered. "They're not working."

"Not that I'm not grateful," Mayhara said, shaking her head, "but why?"

Avi bared his teeth and began stumbling toward them.

"I can't seem to form any particles." Yuki gestured at Mayhara's free hand. "You try. Try to form a rock or something. Anything."

Mayhara's brow furrowed, but she did what Yuki had suggested and lifted her hand, palm up, between them. Her eyes were wide and full of panic. "It's not working. Why isn't it working?"

"Maybe it has something to do with where we are." Yuki looked up at the sky again. The shimmering haze had more of a bluish tint now as it traveled around the sun. "I've only read a little about this realm, and my memory seems to be failing me at the moment."

Avi snarled as he got closer, stumbling and grunting every few steps as he clutched at the wound in his side.

"We need to get away from him, though, just in case. We don't know if this lack of magic is temporary or not." Yuki patted the satchel. "The comet is only a couple of days away. It's needed to destroy Kashmeru. We need to figure out how to get back and get the scroll to the Lotus temple before it's too late."

Mayhara gave Yuki a solid nod, glancing once at the approaching dark mage before taking her hand. They pushed forward, making their way through the puzzle of trees and bushes, unsure of which direction they should be heading. The only thing Yuki knew for sure was it had to be in the direction away from Avi.

Four

Loni adjusted the straps of the backpack she carried to the car. She was used to being on the run, but this was different. There was an urgency that bit at her brain and a lurking sense of doom.

They'd gathered what they could from the house and were almost done packing up the vehicles. Loni was afraid the Pishacha now knew what their cars and Jae's motorcycle looked like and could have the police keep an eye out for them, but they had no other way to get to New Delhi quickly while avoiding being seen in public.

"Then I guess Karina's protection spell didn't work," Shiro said to Mr. Kitaro as they loaded a couple more bags into the trunk of one of the cars. Shiro paused to run a hand through his copper-tipped, black hair. "Since the Pishacha were somehow able to get into the house and take your dagger."

Salina appeared beside the other car, having placed some provisions on one of the seats. She eyed the others.

"We have to remember," Mr. Kitaro answered, "that we do not fully understand what the dark mages are capable of."

"You think they have powers that could undo a witch's spell?" Loni asked.

Salina bit her lip. "That's a scary thought."

"Perhaps not all spells." Mr. Kitaro clapped invisible dust off his hands. "Otherwise, they'd have been able to break the spell sealing Kashmeru's tomb."

Shiro shrugged. "I mean, essentially that's what they're doing. With their magic and the dagger, they'll be breaking a witch's spell."

"No." Mr. Kitaro shook his head. "Not without a witch to reverse the sealing spell. Hence all the fuss about the grimoire."

Loni's attention diverted to Jae, who was tying a duffle bag to his bike with elastic rope. He didn't seem to be paying attention to the conversation. Upon closer inspection, Loni spotted wrinkles worrying his forehead. He'd been far away in thought since they'd found out the other elites and Karina were missing. Though she knew he cared for the safety and well-being of all their missing friends, there was no doubt his heart was hurting most because of Mayhara's absence. And knowing that was tearing a hole in her soul.

Still, she wanted to be there for him. But just as she got up the nerve to speak to him, Darshana appeared and cleared her throat.

"We'll need to depart soon. I can't imagine the Pishacha will grant us any more time than they already have, whatever their plan is."

"I think their plan was to disband us," Shiro said. "And leave us to keep guessing what their next move might be."

Salina crossed her arms. "Well, I'll give them credit. Their tactics are definitely unnerving."

"In any case, I have to agree with Darshana." Mr. Kitaro checked his watch. "We should make haste."

"I could ride up ahead," Jae announced, finally giving the conversation attention. His eyes met Loni's for a mere fraction of a second. "Alone." He cleared his throat. "The bike is packed pretty full. But, uh, I can keep an eye out for what's in front of us. I'll be wearing my earpiece and monitoring traffic updates. I can signal if we need to change our route."

"I can drive one car," Shiro said. "Or at least take the first shift."

"Shifts sound good," Salina agreed. "I'll drive the other one."

"Shotgun." Loni gave her a half-smile.

"I'll accompany our copper elite, then," Mr. Kitaro said.

"I'll ride wherever I fit, I suppose." Darshana gave them all a nod. "Let's say five minutes to grab any last-minute items?"

They all agreed, and though Loni longed to speak to Jae, she instead took the opportunity to double-check her room. She had shared it with Yuki and Penny, and now both of them were missing. Leaving the room now, before anyone knew where they might be, felt strange. Like abandoning them and then jetting off somewhere where they couldn't be found.

"Ready?" Salina asked as she found her in the hallway.

"I guess, yeah."

It wasn't until they were a good half hour into their drive that the nausea and shakes began. Loni kept her eyes on Jae's motorcycle in front of them, wishing to get rid of the acidic taste in her mouth.

Her brain was screaming, *"Moxy!"* And it was taking every ounce of willpower she had to not divert Salina in the direction of her dealer. She already felt guilty for abandoning Yuki and Penny. Her helplessness in losing her sister added to her desperate emotion, and watching Jae—the man who'd broken her heart—ride up ahead of her, knowing his mind was on someone else, just made things worse.

When she let out a shuddered breath, Salina glanced her way.

"Are you all right?"

Loni bit the inside of her cheek. "Fine."

"Loni."

"What?"

"You're not fine. Look at you."

Loni wiped sweat from her brow and dug her nails into her seat. "I'm working through it."

"Okay." Salina glanced her way again, worry etched on her face. "Hey. I'm here, okay? I know we don't exactly have the best history, but we're in this together now. And despite what you might think, I do care about you."

Loni squeezed her seat more tightly as she nodded. Salina's words were like medicine for her heart, but they didn't quite help stop the acid churning in her stomach.

Salina reached out, and Loni took her hand, forcing herself not to dig her nails into Salina's skin.

Up ahead, Jae signaled for them to veer off.

"What's happening now?" Salina muttered, following his directions.

Loni released her hand so she could have better control of the wheel.

Shiro followed behind them as Jae led them into a humble highway rest stop.

Salina parked the car next to Jae's motorcycle and let out a sigh. Shiro pulled up on the other side of the car and glanced their way as he cut his engine. Everyone got out of their cars, and Jae dismounted from his bike. The group gathered around Jae as he removed his helmet.

The rest stop was comprised of a row of parking spots situated along a lonely sidewalk. A small building containing restrooms stood among weeds and unmanicured bushes. A few picnic tables sat in the grass. All but one were unoccupied.

Loni glanced at the group of three young people— probably the same age as her—sitting at the table that was occupied. They were messily dressed and didn't seem to care much about the state of their hair. One of the young women had bloodshot eyes protruding over thick, dark bags. The young man kept bouncing one leg and hunched his shoulders as he glanced around. The other young woman was constantly flicking her lighter on, her cigarette dangling from her dry lips.

Loni couldn't help but think the group was using drugs. It might not have been Moxy they were indulging in, but Loni was sure it was something that could take off the edge. Her mouth filled with saliva, and her hands started to shake. She crossed her arms in an attempt to steady them.

She tried as hard as she could to concentrate on what Jae was saying and ignore the threesome at the picnic table, but she found herself glancing over at them every few seconds.

"The Imperial Police have got road control set up about ten miles up the highway," Jae said, addressing the whole group as they gathered around him. "According to the traffic report, they're set up in intervals all the way from here to New Delhi. We're going to have to take the next exit and stay on the back roads."

"How long is that going to take?" Shiro asked.

"It depends, but definitely longer than we anticipated."

Loni's focus drifted back to the threesome at the picnic tables. They had to be using, she could tell. How easy would it be for her to go over and find out?

"All right," Shiro said. "Sounds like we have no other choice."

"We can manage," Salina put in. "We'll make it."

"Sounds like here's no time to lose, then." Darshana gave Jae a nod. "We'll be right behind you. Let's be on our way."

As they made their way back to the vehicles, Shiro

seemed to take a detour to Jae's bike. Loni couldn't hear what they were saying, but there was an unmistakable sadness in Jae's features when Shiro lightly slapped his back. She tried to listen more intently, but the only clear sentence she heard was, "We'll find her."

Mayhara.

That was where Jae's mind was. She had no doubt about it. Though it tore Loni up inside, she knew Jae's feelings for Mayhara were stronger than anything he'd ever felt for her. Her brain felt numb as she came to terms with it, but there was nothing she could do. She'd lost him.

A far-off siren sounded. Shiro looked over his shoulder at the road. Whatever the source of the siren, it wasn't near. Yet.

Loni watched as the threesome at the picnic table hurriedly gathered their things and scrambled to a rusty, white compact car. She was sure the small plastic bag the young man stuck in his pocket was their drug of choice. Her heart felt as if it were caving in on itself. She told herself to fight off the urge to run up to the man and ask him to sell to her. She didn't even care what it was. She needed something, anything, to stop her suffering.

Shiro ran to his car and climbed in. Jae pulled his helmet on. Salina started the car, but Loni still stood with the passenger side door open.

The threesome closed their door and the car's lights came on.

"Wait," she let out.

Salina ducked into the car and faced her with drawn brows. "What?"

Loni's heart pounded, and her mouth watered. Her head spun from the anguish. She swallowed hard and then shook her head. She had to avoid the temptation. The fate of the world was at stake. No matter how much she wanted to ease her pain, she had to put their mission first. "Never mind. It's nothing. Let's go."

Five

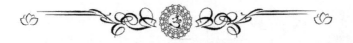

Karina shook out her hands, blowing out shuddered breaths as Rikuto stared her down. He hadn't taken his eyes off her the entire time since they'd been left alone. Though the situation she was in was making her skin crawl, she wished Naree and Bhutano would return from wherever they had escaped to so she wouldn't be alone with Rikuto any longer than she needed to be.

She was relieved when the door to the apartment opened. But instead of Naree and Bhutano returning, another dark mage entered the room. This one had no hair, though he had the same tattoo on his neck as the other dark mages. His face was slim, and he walked with a gangly gait. He only spared Karina a second's glance before traveling over to sit beside Rikuto. In his hands were two small cylindric containers containing some kind of liquid. He handed one to Rikuto.

"Is this from Yung's?" Rikuto asked.

"No. Yung's was out of my way. It's from Sampan."

"Kun, man, Sampan is a rip-off. It's mostly watered-down broth and barely anything else."

"Just shut up and eat, Rikuto. You want Yung's, you can get it yourself."

Rikuto snarled at Kun, but he took the plastic utensil Kun handed him and opened his container, placing the lid on the coffee table.

The delicious scent of oyster sauce and bay leaves wafted through the air. Karina's stomach let out a small gurgle of hunger. She quickly placed her arm over her midsection to quiet the sound. She didn't know if the Pishacha had any intention of feeding her, but she wasn't about to ask the dark mages.

"Your hair's not growing back yet," Rikuto said between slurps. "It's because you're not getting any nutrition from Sampan's soup. You need to go to Yung's."

"It's growing back. Shut up."

"You should have left it like it was. The green suited you. Fit with your whole *poison* persona."

Karina's breath stuck in her throat. *Poison.* This was the dark mage who'd poisoned her grandmother. Who'd ultimately killed her. Karina dug her nails into her palms, forcing herself not to react. Forcing herself not to jump up from the chair and attack him.

You're outnumbered. Stay calm.

She could use a spell, but chances were that Naree would return and use mage powers to take her down. Or she'd make Rikuto slice her throat like he had with Tien Thi.

"It still smells like blood in here," Kun said. "Didn't they get it all?"

"They got most of it," Rikuto answered after another slurp of his soup. "Doesn't matter. We're leaving tomorrow."

"Well, they should have had Harish syphon the blood away with his powers."

"That's not how it works. He syphons magic."

"Witch's blood is magic, isn't it?" Kun let out a chuckle. "He and Daiki still out at the camps? I thought they'd be done setting up the explosives by now."

"Yeah, I think they're almost done." Realizing what they'd just said, Rikuto turned to look at Karina.

Karina kept her head down, pretending not to listen to their banter. When the door opened again, her chin shot up.

Naree practically glided in. She was so graceful; it was as if she were floating. Her eyes locked with Karina's as she continued into the apartment. Behind her was Bhutano in Penny's body, followed by a uniformed Imperial Police officer.

No. Not an officer. A captain. Karina could tell by his uniform. The captain's uniform was grayish blue in color, whereas the police chief's was more of a navy blue. And there were stars above the New United Asia emblem on his chest, which set him apart from the normal Imperial Police officers. It figured Bhutano would pick someone with authority to possess. Karina wondered if this captain was next in line to be the new Chief of Police. Whoever he was, he looked eager to let Bhutano possess his body. Karina almost cringed at the lengths Kashmeru's followers would go to for him. Blindly following an evil god for what had to be an empty promise of immortality.

Bhutano moved slightly slower than the other two, cringing now and then because of the wound in his shoulder. Penny's blouse was tinged with blood, and Karina felt an urgency to heal her.

Karina wrung her hands as the three people who entered the room came over to stand in front of her. She almost forgot Rikuto and Kun were there, until Rikuto sneered at her as he backed away.

"How do you want to do this?" Naree asked Bhutano while sizing up Karina. "The healing first?"

"No." Bhutano locked eyes with Karina. "For all we know, this could be some clever trick where the witch incapacitates me. Or traps my spirit somewhere like she probably did to Avi."

Naree crossed her arms and lifted her chin. It was as if she had already decided Karina was guilty of Bhutano's accusations.

"We'll do the transfer first. Put me in a safe place." Bhutano turned to the police captain and held him by his shoulders. "Are you ready, Captain Kang?"

"It is my honor to serve my god." Kang kept his shoulders squared as he held Bhutano's gaze.

"Kashmeru will reward you in the new world." Bhutano intensified his grip on the captain's shoulders.

When the eyes that were really Penny's glazed over and turned the blackest of blacks, Karina felt her breath leave her body for a moment. She could only gape in disbelief when Penny's jaw dropped and a swarm of black particles emerged from her mouth. It was like an intense cloud of tiny flies floating out between Bhutano and Kang. Karina felt a sharp twist in her stomach watching the scene play out. Kang's mouth then widened, and the black particles moved in a snake-like motion through Kang's lips.

In the next second, Penny's eyes rolled to the back of her head, and she released Kang's shoulders to crumple to the floor. Karina gasped and ran to her, crouching down to gather Penny into her lap.

Captain Kang's eyes also rolled back, but before he could fall, Rikuto and Kun rushed forward to catch him under his arms.

"Take him to the couch," Naree told them. "It usually takes a moment for his spirit to settle in the new host."

Karina swallowed; it was hard to find her voice. "What about Penny?"

Naree shrugged. "We shall see. Perhaps she wasn't strong enough to survive Bhutano leaving her body. Perhaps his presence was the only thing keeping her alive."

Karina's jaw hung open. But Naree ignored her and moved over to observe Captain Kang. She whispered some directions to the dark mages that Karina could not hear.

Karina shifted her focus to Penny's face, pushing her hair away from her eyes, hoping she would wake up. The slow rise and fall of Penny's chest sent a wave of relief through her.

She's alive. But for how long?

Karina moved the material of Penny's shirt aside and peeled back the bloody bandage. The wound was clean; Naree had extrapolated the bits of diamond bullet from Penny's shoulder, but she was still losing a lot of blood.

I can't wait any longer. I need to do this now.

Karina placed a hand over Penny's wound and closed her eyes. Her lips began to move, the whisper of a healing spell barely loud enough for her to hear herself. Her hand began to warm, but she wasn't sure if it was the spell or Penny's blood causing the temperature change.

She repeated the spell once more, just to be sure, before she dared to open her eyes. The glare that was set upon her when she looked up made her flinch. Kun rubbed his chin and scrutinized Penny. Karina averted her eyes and moved her hand away from Penny's wound.

Just as Kun started toward them, Naree spoke up. "He's waking up."

Kun turned away from Karina to join the empress, and in that moment, Penny stirred.

Karina held back a gasp. "Penny," she whispered.

Penny tried to sit up but froze and winced.

"Don't move." Karina put a hand on her elbow. "The bleeding has stopped, but you still need time to—"

Captain Kang stood and stretched out his neck. He flexed his arms and then straightened his uniform.

Karina knew there was no time to lose. She squeezed Penny's elbow tightly and locked eyes with her. Leaning closer, she pushed out her magic and whispered, "Remember."

Penny blinked. "Wh—"

"That's all the time you get," Naree announced,

coming over to stand above them. "You've done all you can do, and now I shall do what I said I would."

Karina wanted to protest, but Naree's glare stopped her. She got to her feet and helped Penny stand up. "You mean you'll release her now."

Naree sighed. "That too, I suppose. I do keep my word. But first, her mind."

Penny's breath shuddered, and she stared wide-eyed at Karina. Karina kept her lips pressed together and squeezed Penny's hand. She wasn't sure if the spell she'd just casted would work, but she had to believe it would.

Naree held out her hand to Penny. Penny visibly swallowed and stepped toward the empress.

"Is this really necessary?" Karina asked.

"We made a deal," Bhutano said through Kang.

Karina wrapped her arms around herself as Naree placed her palms near Penny's temples.

A purple glow emanated from her hands, reflecting off the sides of Penny's face. Karina felt as if the procedure went on forever. She hadn't even known wiping someone's mind was something a mage could do. Penny's eyes went from wide to droopy-lidded, and then Naree pulled her hands away.

Karina waited, watching Penny's face, but her expression remained void of awareness, empty of emotion. She half-expected her to fall to the ground, but Penny simply stood there, like a statue. "What did you do to her?"

"Don't worry." Naree gestured to Rikuto to take Penny's arm. "She's in a sedated state for now, but my dark mages will escort her somewhere safe. Somewhere where she can't cause any trouble."

"How could she cause trouble?" Karina refrained from shouting despite the anger bubbling inside her. "You've erased her memories."

"One can't be too careful," Naree replied. "Especially in times of war."

"Where exactly will they take her?"

Naree smirked. "Do you really think I'd be foolish enough to tell you?" She gestured to her dark mages again, indicating the door.

Kun and Rikuto held each of Penny's arms and led her out of the room. Penny's legs moved her along, but her stoic expression remained. Karina's heart pounded as they disappeared, worry stabbing her like a sharp axe to her chest.

"And now," Naree began, "for your part of the bargain."

Naree pulled a necklace out from the neckline of her blouse. Karina noticed a small key hanging from it. With graceful movements, Naree glided over to a cabinet and unlocked one of the drawers. From it, she pulled out a large, withered book.

The grimoire.

The faded brown leather had a few cracks in it. The spine was a softer material, probably purposely designed so it had more give. The pages were a yellowing parchment, worn at the edges. It smelled of dust and sage.

Karina wiped her sweaty palms on her pants, shifting her feet.

"You might want to get comfortable, dear." Naree tilted her head. "You've got an important spell to learn."

Six

As they traveled farther, Yuki noticed the landscape around them. Their position seemed to be elevated, as if they were on a mountain. In the distance, in one direction, a desert stretched, its sand a soft beige color. In the other direction, there was a lush green forest and a vast, crystal blue lake.

Yuki's mind scrambled as she tried to remember what she might have learned about the spirit realm. She knew it was a parallel plane that existed with their world, sort of overlapping with it. But she couldn't recall much else. Her mind insisted, however, that if there was a way in, then there had to be a way out.

Luckily, they seemed to have lost Avi. For now. She knew he was persistent and would stop at nothing to get to them. Though she couldn't be too sure he'd survive his injuries much longer.

"How do you know where to go?"

Yuki was roused from her thoughts. She looked over her shoulder at Mayhara, who seemed to be struggling to keep up with her. "Sorry, what?"

"You seem to be leading us as if you know exactly where we're supposed to go."

The statement made Yuki stop. She turned to face Mayhara full on and blinked for a minute in confusion.

Mayhara's deep brown eyes were wide, obviously still shaken by the fact that they were trapped here. Their constant movement and the humidity in the air turned her usual silky, brunette waves into a bit of a thick, frizzy mess. But Yuki had to admit, she was still beautiful despite it all.

Mayhara adjusted the strap of the satchel as she fought to keep her balance.

"I don't know," Yuki finally said. "I guess I just feel… a pull."

"A pull to where?"

"I'm not sure. But I know it's right."

The tiniest of smiles came to life on Mayhara's face. "Okay. I trust you."

Yuki reached out and gave her hand a squeeze. "I'm sorry I got us into this mess."

"What? No. You probably saved my life. Both of our lives. If you hadn't tried to get us away from Avi, we could be dead right now."

Something pink with transparent green wings fluttered by Yuki's ear. When she tried to swat it away, it flitted over to her other ear, buzzing incessantly. "I'm not entirely sure we *aren't* dead right now."

Mayhara let out a laugh as they continued to walk. "I thought you read up on this place when we attended the academy. Wasn't it on the course requirements for diamond mages?"

Yuki pushed past a bush with glowing lilac flowers. "Well, I mean, I guess it was more theoretical. Because who would be able to get information on this place without actually coming here?"

"A skilled diamond mage, maybe? Or an amethyst mage might have seen it? Or… Darshana."

Yuki huffed a laugh. "True. She probably knows all about this place. Oh, watch your step here."

Mayhara looked through the fog where Yuki had gestured. Rocks and pebbles were embedded in the soil. The uneven land was riddled with dips and holes and slants that could make even the most graceful walker stumble. Mayhara had already remarked on what terrible timing it was that she couldn't use her earth-manipulating powers to make their journey easier.

"So, what *did* you learn about this place?" Mayhara asked, her hand tight on the strap of the bag.

"Well, mainly that it was created by a rupture in the cosmic and communal coherence. You know the Yin and Yang?"

"Of course."

"So it's like that space in between. Yang is the manifested side of existence, and Yin is the side yet to be. The hidden, or the potential of life. So the spirit realm is sort of like that plane connecting the two."

"So is it like purgatory?" Mayhara asked. "The plane between Earth and heaven?"

"Would it help you if I said, 'yes and no'?"

Mayhara chuckled. "No, but I wouldn't expect a more fitting answer when it comes to this stuff."

"Right?" Yuki smiled at her.

"So, since it's the spirit realm, does that mean there are actual spirits here?"

"That's the theory. But to be honest, I don't think anyone has testified to having proof. Like, even the few people who've experienced death for a couple of minutes before they were revived, they've talked about seeing a light. Probably that." She pointed to the sun. "And maybe hearing voices of loved ones they lost. But honestly, who's to say?"

For a small moment, Yuki allowed herself to imagine discovering her parents here. They'd been killed when she'd run away from the government, and she'd never had any closure when she'd found out they were dead. She pushed down the feeling of hope, however, not wanting to eventually face disappointment.

"Well, if it's any consolation," Mayhara said, "I'm glad we're together here. Not alone."

The snapping of a branch caused them to freeze.

"Speaking of not being alone..." Yuki swallowed.

Cutting through the fog, Avi hobbled toward them. Yuki wasn't sure how he'd managed to catch up, but there was no time to deliberate.

She and Mayhara took off, trying their best not to trip and fall because of the bumpy terrain. They had to dodge a few prickly bushes that popped up in their path. The fog seemed to grow thicker, swirling around them as they ran.

Yuki heard Mayhara grunt and looked over her shoulder. "You okay?"

"Fine," she answered between breaths. "The strap of the satchel ripped on a branch or something. Keep going."

They picked up their pace, and at one point, Mayhara managed to get in front of Yuki, holding the satchel in her hand.

The fog thinned a bit, and Yuki could just make out the ground below their feet. Or, in their case, the lack thereof.

"Wait! Stop!" She reached out and grabbed Mayhara by her arm.

They skidded to a stop just in time. But in Mayhara's effort to right herself, the satchel slipped from her grasp.

Directly in front of their toes, the earth fell away. They stood at the edge of a cliff, and though they were safe at the top, the satchel containing the scroll plummeted down into the abyss.

"No!" Mayhara futilely reached for it. Yuki had to pull her back.

Yuki risked looking over the edge, tracking where the satchel had gone. As it dropped, it dispersed the fog around it. She was sure it was a hundred-meter drop at least, but she watched it land near a tree with bright red flowers.

Mayhara let out a curse. "There must be a way down. Other than this, I mean."

Yuki heard a rustle behind them. "Avi's gaining ground." She quickly glanced around and spotted something that might help. "Look!"

They backed away from the cliff and found wide, stone steps that appeared to descend in a curve around the mountain. But there was a large gap—an empty space that dropped into a low ditch—between where they stood and where the steps began.

"We'll need to jump for it," Mayhara said. She seemed to be calculating the distance. "We can make it. I doubt

Avi can. Not with his injuries."

Yuki felt skeptical, but there was no time to lose. "Okay, let's do it."

Avi neared, sneering at them.

They took off running for the gap. Yuki held her breath as they pushed off into a jump. She let out an *oomph* as she landed. Her legs felt sore and she'd hit her knee against the stone, but they'd done it. They'd cleared the gap.

They stood on the stone steps, finding their bearings, and turned back to face Avi. He clutched his side, soaked in blood and surveilling the gap. He was in no condition to jump it, and he knew it. Yuki locked eyes with him as he backed away. She was sure he was searching for an alternative route to get to them.

With labored breaths, she placed a hand on Mayhara's arm. "Okay, let's go find that satchel."

Seven

The words on the page began to blur. Karina had been staring at them for hours. She wanted to close the book and rest her eyes, but she was being watched. Though not intently watched anymore. It was just Kun and Rikuto in the room with her, left by Naree and Bhutano, who had made it clear they had things to prepare. After the dark mages bored their gazes into her for twenty minutes, they slowly lost interest, resorting to checking their Linqs and not really paying attention to her. After all, the only thing she'd been doing was reading one solitary page of a book.

She had to admit when Naree had first put the grimoire in front of her, she'd been fascinated by it. The moment she'd touched it, her fingers had tingled from the thought of the centuries of witches who'd written in it. She'd run her hand over the words, half-afraid her fingers would make the ink smear. It was a relief when she found she was able to read the ancient language it was written in, but the thought of releasing Kashmeru from his tomb and unleashing pure evil upon the world caused her skin to crawl. The spell she was learning the words of was the spell that had locked Kashmeru in his tomb, a spell cast by a very powerful witch. Karina's job was to learn the spell so she could undo it, to basically turn the spell on its head and break the bond.

She desperately wanted to flip the pages, to see what else might be in the book, and maybe figure out how to use the small scroll that had disappeared with Mayhara and Yuki. Information that would only be useful if they would somehow return from wherever she'd accidentally sent them.

She held the corner of the page and eyed the dark mages. Would they notice if she were to flip the page? They weren't even looking her way. Her pulse thrummed faster as she got her nerve up to peel the page back. But as soon as she lifted the page, the door to the apartment opened. Karina quickly smoothed down the page and shifted in her seat. The two dark mages lounging in the living room straightened up, tucking their Linqs away.

Karina expected Naree and Bhutano to return, but instead, the female dark mage stomped into the room. She was thin and fast. Her dark hair hung to just above her shoulders, and her eyes were like black coal.

"Hey, Ru. Think fast." Rikuto threw something at her head.

Karina didn't register what the object was until Ru used her powers to stop it in midair.

Ru had her hand raised, and when she twisted her wrist, the crumpled ball of metal turned. With a flick of her hand, the metal ball shot back in Rikuto's direction. He let out a playful *ugh* as it hit him in the stomach.

"You here to relieve us of our watch?" Kun asked.

"Yeah." The annoyed frown didn't leave her face. "It was supposed to be Harish and Daiki, but they're not back from the Kadma prison camp yet."

"Gods, how many more camps do they need to boobytrap?" Rikuto asked, tossing the metal ball into the air and catching it before it hit him in the face.

"Kadma's the last one, I think. They've been busy hitting the others all day." Ru plopped down on the couch next to Kun, casting a glance at Karina.

Karina couldn't stop looking at her. The image of Ru at Police Chief Lin's funeral when her mother—Director Shei—had died in her arms held strong in her mind, along with the haunting look in Ru's eyes that had spoken of pure vengeance.

Ru scowled. "What are you looking at?"

Karina almost dropped her gaze, but a little voice inside her head told her to stay strong, to not show weakness.

Ru stood, not breaking eye contact. "What is it?" She squared her jaw and took two steps toward Karina.

Karina couldn't help but think of Qiang. She remembered the look of deep concern on Shiro's face when he'd told her that Qiang had been ultimately responsible for Director Shei's death. "Nothing."

Ru narrowed her eyes. "I don't believe you."

Karina forced herself to keep her chin up. "It's just… I recognize you. From the funeral that was on the news."

Ru searched her face. "And?"

Karina tried to hold her gaze. "That's it. Nothing else."

"Why don't I believe you?"

Karina shook her head. "It doesn't matter."

Ru raised her hand. The crumpled piece of metal Rikuto had thrown at her earlier jetted through the air and stopped a mere inch from Karina's left eye. Karina gasped but held still. A jagged point sticking out from the metal ball taunted her iris.

"Does it matter now?" Ru sneered.

Karina swallowed hard and tried not to shake.

"I know there's something you're not telling me," Ru insisted. "I know that look."

"No." Karina's gaze was locked on the metal ball.

"It has something to do with that day, doesn't it?"

The metal ball shifted closer. Karina didn't dare to blink.

"Tell me!" Ru shouted. "What do you know?"

Karina almost shook her head, but the metal ball hovered closer. For the life of her, she couldn't think of a spell to get out of the situation.

"It's about whoever killed my mother, isn't it?"

Karina was only vaguely aware of Kun and Rikuto, who came to stand beside Ru as the drama unfolded.

"I bet it was her," Rikuto said, his arms crossed over his chest.

"No." Karina's breath was shaky. "It wasn't me."

"But you know who it was." Ru came closer, but Karina couldn't look past the ball. "Tell me who it was."

Karina bit her lip, refusing to speak.

Ru twisted her wrist.

Faster than Karina could track, the metal ball swooped across her cheek. She hadn't even realized it had sliced her skin until the ball returned to its spot in front of her eye and the hot sting of the cut began to burn.

"Let's try that again," Ru said. "And this time, I won't miss. Who killed my mother?"

Karina let out a shuddered breath.

"You know who it is!" Ru screamed. "Tell me."

"It… It was the extremist leader. I… I don't know if he pulled the trigger, but it was his call." Karina felt like a traitor for telling her. Tears welled up in her eyes.

"He's part of the group that escaped from the camps, right?" Kun asked.

The metal ball dropped into Karina's lap as Ru turned away from her. Ru was shaking, her hands balled into fists. The dark mages and Karina flinched as Ru let out a guttural scream.

Ru charged for the door.

"Wait," Rikuto called after her. "Where are you going?"

Ru threw the door open and glared back at them. "They'll pay for this. This extremist leader and all of his followers. They'll pay. My mother will be avenged!"

❦

The road before them seemed to blur. Darshana's breath left her for a moment. It felt as if a boulder had just barreled into her chest. She reached out with shaking hands to grasp the dashboard. She had to hold on to something for fear of tipping over, even if she was strapped in place by her seatbelt.

Shiro glanced at her from the driver's seat. "Darshana, what is it?"

"Something has happened. Something horrible. I feel… death. A lot of death."

Shiro's eyes were wide, and he visibly swallowed. He looked in the rearview mirror at Mr. Kitaro.

"Nothing's showing up on any of the news sites," Mr. Kitaro announced as he checked his Linq.

"Yet," Darshana put in. "It's only now happened."

"Do you think it's Mayhara and the others?" Shiro asked. The color seemed to be draining from his face.

"I can't be sure. I'm feeling very weak." She placed her hands on the sides of her head and tried to steady her breathing.

"Do you want me to pull over so you can get some air?" Shiro asked.

Darshana looked up at the road. Everything seemed to be swaying in her vision. The sun was setting, sprays of orange and pink streaked across the sky. It would be dark soon.

"Where are we, exactly?" she asked.

Shiro checked the navigation screen. "Just outside Sainipura."

"So far off course," Darshana remarked.

"It was the only way to avoid the roadblocks, unfortunately."

The back roads they'd been taking had slowed their progress tremendously. It shouldn't have taken more than a day to get to New Delhi, even in heavy traffic. If this was the enemy's way of keeping them from interfering with their plan to bring back Kashmeru, it seemed to be working.

"Oh my word," Mr. Kitaro suddenly said.

"What?" Shiro asked, glancing in the rearview mirror. "What is it?"

"The prison camps. News is coming in that bombs are going off everywhere."

Shiro's hands seemed to slip from the steering wheel. As he fought to get control of the car, Darshana braced herself. Not just from the movement, but from the confirmation of the deaths she felt. Such an enormous loss of mage life. She pressed a hand to her chest and fought off the ache.

"Pull over," Mr. Kitaro suggested, holding his Linq to his ear. "I'll tell the others."

Darshana's heart was still racing when they all

gathered at the side of the road. Everyone was desperately checking their Linqs to see if they could find out more information.

"Not all the camps were affected," Salina said, her eyes glued to her screen. "Maybe half."

"For now," Shiro put in, pacing so much he was sure to wear a hold in the ground.

"Darshana." Loni squeezed her hands. "My parents."

"I don't see their camp listed as one of the ones that were attacked," she answered.

"But we don't know if the attacks have stopped yet, do we?" Jae tucked away his Linq and raked his fingers through his hair.

"No, we don't." Darshana glanced at the moon. Night was coming fast. "We can't worry about it here on the side of the road. We need to take shelter. I know a place not too far from here. A sanctuary where we can take rest for the night." Darshana ran her hands down the sides of her face, trying to fight off the dizziness. "We'll be safe, and I can regain my strength. We can all re-energize before tomorrow."

"Okay." Shiro readied the car key, prepared to move on. "Name the place."

Darshana nodded. "I'll type it into the navigation system. Jae, Salina, you can follow us. It's our turn to lead."

Eight

Salina couldn't get the recent, shocking news out of her head. The prison camps had been destroyed. Not all of them, thank the gods, but about half. Shiro had obviously freaked out at the news. She'd gotten a fright when he'd seemed to have lost control of his car.

Thankfully, it didn't take long for the news sites to put

out a list of the prison camps that were not affected, and once the list was public, Darshana assured Loni both her parents as well as Mayhara's family were safe. The bad news was they weren't sure the attacks had stopped for good, and reporters on every channel were saying the authorities believed the explosions to be the work of the extremists.

The mages had known this would be coming. Jae had overheard the governor talking about it with Director Shei. It was a setup devised by the government and put into action by the Pishacha. Shiro had said Qiang and his gang were doing everything they could to deactivate the bombs, but they apparently hadn't been able to get to them all in time. Salina's heart hurt for all the lost mages and mage families massacred by such a ruthless act.

Once they were over their initial shock, Darshana had insisted they continue on their way to the sanctuary she'd told them about. The sun had already set, the sky beginning to twinkle with stars. The comet appeared to be almost directly above them. Darshana doubted they'd be able to make much progress on the unreliable back roads at night.

Now, at their destination, Salina grunted, lugging her

duffle bag over the rocky terrain. They'd parked the cars near an abandoned construction site and had had to walk the whole way to what Darshana had described as a sanctuary for the night.

At first, it appeared as though they were going to be hiding out in the woods. Or perhaps in a cave. Salina shuddered at the thought. The last thing she needed was a run-in with a wolf. But then the tents appeared. It seemed like a hundred of them, in various muted colors, and each one large enough to hold a fairly large-sized family. A few caravans were set up, adorned with small flags and paper lanterns.

"Are these…" Shiro looked as though he wasn't sure how to continue. "This camp. Is it a travelers' camp?"

"Travelers?" Salina's brows scrunched up. "As in… Roma?"

"Roma?" Loni scanned the area. "You mean Romani? Like, what some people used to call 'gyp—'"

"Don't say it," Jae interrupted her. "It's considered offensive. But to your point, I thought the Romani people were from Europe."

Darshana placed her hands together. "The Roma's roots are actually Northern Indian in origin. The Punjab region, to be precise. They traveled to Europe around the eighth century. And the term used to describe them came to be because the Europeans thought the people were from Egypt."

"So we were both mistaken," Jae said. "The Europeans and me."

"There's someone coming toward us," Shiro announced.

Everyone straightened and turned toward the two men walking their way. The older of the two had hair as white as Darshana's. One would never be able to tell his age from his physique, however. From the looks of him, if he wasn't a weightlifter, he must have gotten his muscle training from pulling trees out of the ground with his bare hands. His laugh lines were deep when he smiled. The younger of the two shared most of the same features: angled cheek bones, strong, square jaw, and contagious smiles. They had to be related. His thick, dark hair hung to his earlobes in a shaggy, carefree way that was just mysterious enough to be sexy. And he looked just as built as his older counterpart.

Salina couldn't help but notice how chiseled his jawline was. When the young man met her gaze, she felt a flash of heat erupt on her cheeks and neck.

"Darshana," the older man said with a bow. "It's been many years."

"One might even say decades." Darshana appeared to be holding back a smirk.

She bowed in return, and then they both smiled as he pulled her into a hug.

"Patrin." Darshana pulled back and looked him over. "You look well. Camp life suits you. Always has."

"Says the woman who's somehow managed to slow down the effects of time." Patrin let out a low chuckle. He released her and slapped the back of the young man next to him. "This is my grandson, Vano."

Darshana touched her fingers against her mouth for a second. "What? Little Vano? Last time I saw you, you were barely cutting teeth. I remember that little wet rag you'd suck on to ease the pain. You carried it everywhere."

Vano's smile was hypnotic, his teeth perfect, and his lips accentuated by dimples on either side. "As long as you're done breaking out the embarrassing stories, welcome to the camp." When he bowed, his hair fell like a curtain of black silk across his face.

"Thank you, Vano." Darshana's eyes went to Patrin.

"He reminds me of you."

"I'll take that as a compliment." Patrin's gaze traveled to the others in their group. "What brings you our way, Darshana?"

She pursed her lips and took in a long breath. "I need to be honest with you. Our presence here could be dangerous for your people."

A shadow fell over Patrin's face. "Are you being followed?"

"We haven't seen anyone, but we can't be too sure. You know of the Pishacha?"

He straightened his back. "From the prophesy. Yes, I know. The time has come, hasn't it?"

"It has." Darshana glanced beside her, gesturing to each one in the group. "These are a few of the elite mages: Jae, the sapphire elite; Salina, the golden elite; Loni, the emerald elite; and Shiro, the copper elite. And this is Satoshi Kitaro, probably the last of the remaining Sacred Keys."

Patrin bowed to them, and then he stuck out his hand to Mr. Kitaro. "It's a pleasure to meet you."

Mr. Kitaro gave him a slight bow in return and shook his hand. "Likewise, of course."

"We don't mean to cause any trouble," Darshana continued. "We are on our way to meet our fate and prevent Kashmeru's return, but we need a sanctuary for the night to regain our strength before… well, before it all transpires."

"Yes, of course. You are all welcome to stay."

"We can pitch in," Darshana added, "in return for your hospitality."

"Please, Darshana." Patrin placed a gentle hand on her shoulder. "You are about to go into battle to save the world. I'd say it is we who owe you."

"I'll get some tents prepared," Van said. He mirrored his grandfather's earlier gesture by slapping a hand on his grandfather's back. "It's nice to meet you all," he said to them. "I'll let my mother know we'll need extra servings for dinner."

Vano's eyes fell on Salina once more before he turned and ran off to do what he'd said.

"You can follow me," Patrin said. "We've just started a fire."

"Sounds lovely," Darshana said, sidling up beside him as he led the way.

Patrin rubbed one of his ears. "Darshana, I thought

there were supposed to be seven elite."

"There are." Darshana wrung her hands. "The other three have turned up missing. We were all together, and some unknown events took place… I can sense they are in danger, or lost, but I have no way of knowing where they are. And I haven't exactly had the time or peace of mind to meditate and lock in on their location."

"Perhaps a hot meal and a warm fire will help."

"Perhaps."

They hiked for another minute until they reached the center of the camp. It felt more homey here, the tents bigger and more colorful. There were campers parked here and there, and people walked around, dressed in the most fascinating garb, led by small torches that were lit along paths. Word must have traveled fast about their arrival because the people gave them smiles and nods. Or maybe they all recognized Darshana.

Patrin led them to the campfire, where several people were seated. Not too far away, others were preparing food.

"Wait here," Patrin said. "I'll make sure everything is getting set up."

Darshana gave him a small bow as he backed away.

Shiro set down the bags he carried and pulled out his

Linq. Off to the side, Loni and Jae seemed immersed in conversation, each of them scanning the area.

Salina untangled herself from her backpack and set it on the ground. The campfire was mesmerizing. A young teenage boy was stoking it, trying to get the flames higher. Salina held her hand out, her palm already glowing gold. In a matter of seconds, the fire crackled and roared, burning hotter and higher. The teenage boy smiled, his eyes wide with wonder.

Next to her, Darshana shot her a look, one brow raised and the hint of a smirk on her lips.

"I just wanted to help," Salina said to her.

Darshana nodded. "It's very generous of them to let us stay here tonight."

"How do you know Patrin? If you don't mind me asking."

"Believe it or not, our mothers were best friends."

"Really?"

"As children, Patrin and I were always dragged along whenever they would meet up. Our friendship went through many phases through the years growing up. From playground buddies to sworn enemies to secret conspirators—"

"To boyfriend and girlfriend?" Salina nudged her with her elbow.

Darshana let out a chuckle. "I do suspect that Patrin once had feelings for me, and I did find myself desperately longing to be in his company one summer. But I'm afraid our feelings never matched up, timewise. The opportunity was missed on both accounts, and I had to assume it was never meant to be."

"So now you're just friends."

"Old friends. Yes, of course. He moved on, married, had children, and now grandchildren. And I—" Her eyes wandered to Mr. Kitaro for a moment. "I was busy training the empire's finest army."

Salina followed Darshana's gaze, wondering if there was a chance Darshana and Mr. Kitaro would end up together. That was, once they survived the showdown with Kashmeru.

Vano suddenly appeared next to them. "Darshana, the tents are ready."

Darshana placed a hand on his bicep. "Thank you, my boy."

For a second, Salina was disappointed that she hadn't thought to thank him in the same manner.

DIAMOND *Mage*

She should have been asleep hours ago, but sleep simply wouldn't come. It wasn't because of the sleeping bag, which was surprisingly comfortable. And it wasn't because of the unusual surroundings. The tents were magnificently decorated. The hanging tapestries seemed to resemble a mixture of Bohemian and Chinese roots, a blend of vibrant colors and appealing patterns. She didn't mind the smell of earth and grass. In fact, in some ways, it reminded her of her homeland of Eritrea.

What kept her awake was the fact that they were about to fight to the death in the most important battle the world had ever seen. It made her think about how she'd landed in this position. She couldn't help but think about Huojin, her best friend. How it should have been Huojin on the front line with the other elites. But she'd been killed by a dark mage, and Salina had never even had a chance to say goodbye.

Her throat was suddenly parched. She did her best not to make any noise as she got up. She didn't want to wake

Loni or Darshana, who slept not too far away from her spot. As she exited the tent, she hoped she'd be able to find some water.

The fire was still going, though significantly smaller now. Sitting alone, staring into the flames, was Vano. He looked up and her as she approached, and a friendly smile appeared on his face as he stood.

"You're still awake?" she asked quietly.

"Darshana said you were in danger. Someone should keep watch." He tilted his head. "What's kept you up?"

"Destiny, I suppose."

He smirked. "Oh?"

She couldn't help but laugh. "I mean, my destiny. As an elite mage. And how it's time to face it."

"You want to talk about it?"

"Actually, I'd really like some water."

He nodded. "Oh, sure. Of course."

He walked over to a tree stump near the tent and dipped a ladle into a bucket of water. After pouring the water into a clay cup, he handed it to her.

"Thank you."

He watched her as she drank.

She let out a small laugh. "What?"

"Sorry." He seemed to be blushing. "Was I staring?"

"A little."

"Well, at the risk of being too forward, I have to say I'm a bit mesmerized by your beauty."

Her skin grew warm. "Oh. Um, thank you. I, uh, I don't know what to say."

"I don't mean to embarrass you. But, um, look." He pulled out the thin, gold chain that hung around his neck until the pendant at the end was out of his shirt. "This belonged to my grandmother."

"Gold topaz," Salina remarked.

"Yes." He held the topaz in his palm. "That's what your eyes remind me of."

She studied his face for a moment. He was very handsome. And so kind. What was she doing?

"If you're trying to distract me from my worries, I think it might be working."

His smile lit up his face. "We can sit by the fire for a while, if you want. Until you feel tired, I mean. I could use the company."

"Sure." She cradled the cup of water in her hands. "I'd like that."

She wasn't sure how long they'd been talking for, but

it must have been hours. He kept making her laugh, and she kept the fire going. They spoke about topic after topic—all the while with Vano being a perfect gentleman—until her yawns got the best of her and she decided to turn in.

She silently crept back into the tent, knowing that she probably wouldn't get much sleep before they had to get up. But in her mind, it was worth it.

As she slipped back into her sleeping bag, Loni shifted.

"Where were you?" Loni's voice was quiet and slow, as if she'd just woken up.

"I couldn't sleep. I was talking with Vano."

She couldn't be sure, but she thought Loni giggled. "Are you tired now?"

"Exhausted." Salina settled down on her pillow. "How are you?"

Loni didn't answer right away. "What do you mean?"

"I know you were struggling today."

Again, Loni took a second to answer. "I'm doing better. I'm so relieved my parents are okay. For now."

"I'm glad too. I also noticed you speaking with Jae earlier. How are things there?"

"Complicated. But… I guess I'm learning to let him

go. I've fooled myself long enough. He loves Mayhara. I have to stop denying it. Besides, we'll probably all be dead tomorrow."

"Loni!"

"Too dark?" Loni let out a small laugh. "Sorry. Darkness has always been my way of dealing with things."

They were quiet for a while, and Salina thought Loni might have drifted off to sleep again.

"I don't really mean it," Loni finally said. "I don't think it's the end of us. I keep hearing my sister's voice in my head telling me that I'm here for a reason. That I'm meant to fight this battle. And that we'll win."

Salina breathed in a deep breath and slowly exhaled. "For all our sakes, I hope your sister is right."

Nine

Karina pushed around the food on her plate, her mind swirling with the words of the spell Naree had made her learn. Now that she'd spent all day reading it, she felt confident that she'd be able to perform the spell when the time came. The problem was she hated the prospect of releasing a monster.

If only she could look through the grimoire to see what else it contained. Maybe there were clues about how to stop the Pishacha, or maybe she could find information about the small scroll. She still hadn't been able to open it—back when it had been in her possession. If Mayhara and Yuki found their way back with it, she wanted to be ready.

But the grimoire was locked away. When the sun had set earlier, Naree had closed the book and used the key that hung on a necklace she wore to lock the grimoire in a cabinet in the living room. Then Bhutano had thrown Karina in one of the penthouse's guest rooms and locked her in as well. An hour later, a Pishacha soldier had stepped into the room and tossed a plate of food on the dresser for her. His eyes had only met hers for a split second before he'd turned and left the room again. The sound of the lock pad's lock engaging after he'd left still sounded in her mind.

She'd let the food sit for well over an hour now, with no intention of eating anything they gave her. Fear that they might try to drug her or poison her had crossed her mind, but eventually, she gave in. She had only eaten enough to stop her stomach from grumbling. Thoughts about the grimoire and what else it might contain kept her from finishing the meal. She needed to see what else was in the book, but in order to do that, she'd need to get out of the room.

Using a spell to disengage the lock wouldn't be a problem, but she would have to wait until no one was around. She knew they were preparing to leave in the morning to head to the Lotus temple, but she couldn't be sure anyone was still in the apartment. It had been hours, and she suspected that even the goddess Lakshmi had to get her rest before an eventful day.

A whisper touched her ears. She couldn't be sure, but she thought it might have been her grandmother's voice. And though she couldn't clearly make out the words, she was suddenly struck with the memory of a spell her grandmother had once taught her. It was a spell her grandmother had used in the swamps to avoid running into any wild animals or snakes when they were out gathering herbs and plants. A motion sensor spell. If Karina used it, she'd be able to feel if anyone was nearby. It was her best bet to getting to the cabinet unnoticed to get the book.

She paced the room, trying to decide if she should wait

a bit longer. It would be easier to move through the apartment if everyone was asleep.

Her heart thumped in her chest and her palms were damp with sweat. She tried to control her breathing as she went to the door and pressed her ear against it. Not hearing any movement, she straightened her back and called to mind the words of Amalia's spell.

Her fingers tingled as the spell began to work. It was as if her fingers were inching their way under the door and down the hall, splitting up to search the different rooms. In a matter of seconds, she knew that Naree was asleep in her room and Bhutano was smoking on the balcony of his bedroom. One Pishacha soldier—probably he one who'd delivered her plate of food—stood guard outside the apartment door. She couldn't sense the dark mages anywhere and wondered briefly if their powers made it possible to dodge her sensing spell. Though she couldn't be sure if they were in the apartment or not, she couldn't wait any longer to try to get a peek at the grimoire.

Placing her hand on the lock pad, she recited a spell to disengage the lock. Within seconds, the red indicator light switched to green. She blinked in surprise. Usually, it took more effort. She hoped the small beep that sounded was quiet enough not to be heard by the others.

With her hand on the doorknob, she held her breath so she could hear more clearly. Everything was quiet.

Her steps were light as she slipped out of the room and made her way down the dark hall toward the living room. The moonlight shone in through the large windows in the living room, lighting her way in the dark.

She reached out with the sensing spell again to make sure no one was coming. Both Naree and Bhutano were still in their rooms, and the Pishacha remained at his station. Focused on the cabinet that held the grimoire, Karina crept closer.

She could practically hear the grimoire calling to her. Glancing over her shoulder, just in case, she blew out a nervous breath and then turned to focus on the keyhole of the cabinet. Though the spell to get a mechanical lock to disengage usually took a minute to work, the lock clicked open almost as soon as she touched it.

Grandmother, she thought, *your powers are amazing*.

As quietly as she could manage to be, Karina pulled open the cabinet and placed her hands on the grimoire. She might have imagined it, but it felt as if the grimoire clung to her. Like it was longing to be held by a family member. As she opened the book, she realized the moonlight wasn't enough for her to be able to read the pages. Grabbing one of the candles decorating a side table, she whispered the spell to create a flame on the wick. She held the book close and scanned the pages near the trapping spell.

A few pages after the spell, she noticed ragged parchment close to the inside spine.

Someone tore out the page, she whispered to herself.

Though she couldn't be sure, she guessed it was the spell that was rolled up in the small scroll. Someone had gone to great lengths to remove it and secure it elsewhere.

She turned back one page and read the text, her mind translating the words. She couldn't be sure, but she believed one word to translate into *poison*. Could the key to destroying Kashmeru lie in some kind of poison? Was the small scroll some kind of recipe to create a poison strong enough to destroy a god?

The sound of footsteps found her ears. It was soon followed by a low voice Karina could only assume was the Pishacha soldier standing guard outside the apartment. Closing the book, Karina blew out the candle and hurried to return the grimoire to the cabinet. She barely had time to spell the lock closed before she dropped down to hide behind a chair. It was the same chair she'd sat in all day while studying the trapping spell.

A door opened. Karina held her breath.

"How many of the camps were destroyed?"

It was Kun's voice. Karina held her hands over the sides of her neck in an attempt to quiet her heart pounding in her ears.

"About half," Ru answered, "judging from the reports coming in from the wardens."

"Half?"

"Quiet, Kun." This time it was Rikuto speaking.

"What happened to the others?" Kun asked in a quieter voice. "I thought Harish and Daiki set explosives to go off in *all* the camps."

"They did," Ru answered. "They don't know what went wrong. But half is better than none."

Karina hunkered down lower and bit on her fingertips. She knew from Shiro that Qiang and his gang had been busy dismantling the explosives in most of the camps. This discussion told her that Qiang had only managed to get to half the locations.

"I thought the bombs were supposed to be detonated

tomorrow before the ceremony," Kun said.

"I convinced them to detonate them early," Ru replied. "They make me sick. The extremists. All of them. After what they did to my mother, I couldn't let them win. They got what they deserved."

Karina dropped her head into her hands. Half the mage population. Dead. A shudder ran through her body. This was her fault. If she hadn't triggered Ru into destroying the camps early, maybe Qiang and his gang would have had enough time to deactivate all the explosives.

She lowered her head, dread hanging over her like a heavy blanket, and waited until the dark mages were gone so she could sneak back to her room.

Ten

The night air felt cooler, and the ever-present mist snaked its way higher up their legs. Yuki was exhausted after their long climb down the stone steps, which had been made more difficult when the sun had set. A part of her was relieved that the concept of day and night was something that existed in the spirit realm. It gave her a small sense of normalcy in an otherwise mysterious place.

"Did you see where it landed?" Mayhara asked. "If my powers were working, I'd feel the ground so we could find it quicker."

Yuki pointed to a tree with bright red flowers hanging in a cascading, vine-like fashion. "I think it landed by that tree. I'm sure if we feel around in that fog, we'll be able to find it."

"We'll need to hurry, though." Mayhara checked behind them. "I have a feeling Avi might have found another way down the mountain."

They neared the tree and crouched down, stretching their arms out into the low, creeping fog. Yuki couldn't be sure of everything she was touching. There were definitely rocks, grass, and unfortunately prickly plants, but she didn't feel the satchel. Mayhara appeared to be having the same lack of good luck.

A sudden staccato yelp echoed around them. Yuki straightened and scanned the area. It was hard to see, but something quick and white darted toward them. Yuki let out a scream and instinctively moved toward Mayhara.

"What is that?" Mayhara asked.

The creature hopped through the mist, and Yuki grabbed Mayhara's arm.

"I don't know. It's hopping around like a rabbit, but it's quicker and much bigger."

"Just stay still. If it doesn't feel threatened by us, it won't have any reason to attack us."

Yuki did as Mayhara said, forcing herself not to move a muscle as the animal sniffed around in the fog.

A white tail emerged as it continued its search. And then another. And another. Yuki blinked in confusion.

"I think it's a fox," Mayhara whispered.

"But it's practically the size of a dog. And those tails."

Suddenly, the animal stopped. As it lifted its head, Yuki had to admit it looked like a white fox. The fox wiggled its nose as it studied them. More tails lifted from behind it in the fog.

"Nine tails," Mayhara whispered. "It's a *kitsune*."

"Whoa." A small smile formed on Yuki's face. "It's actually really cute."

As her fear dissolved, her curiosity took over and she took a step toward the kitsune.

With a flinch, the kitsune bared its teeth at them. In the next second, it ducked its head into the fog and quickly resurfaced with a strap seized in its mouth.

Mayhara gasped. "The satchel!"

As soon as she'd said it, the kitsune jumped up and scurried off through the fog.

"No!" Yuki didn't even hesitate. She chased after the kitsune, not caring where her feet landed.

"Yuki, wait!"

She was barely aware of Mayhara running behind her. The only thing that mattered was getting the satchel back. There was no telling what their chances were of escaping the spirit realm, but without the small scroll, they were doomed.

The kitsune raced into a meadow, its assemblage of furry white tails bouncing along behind it. The top tips of wildflowers in the field swayed in the fog as the kitsune made its way through. It was way too fast for Yuki, but she wasn't about to give up. The kitsune reached the end of the meadow and froze when a whistle sounded in the air. With its tails wagging, the fox trotted toward a giant oak and disappeared from view.

"Is it gone?" Mayhara asked between labored breaths.

Yuki didn't have enough air in her lungs to answer. Instead, she pointed to the oak and slowed to a walk.

Mayhara caught up and joined her as they rounded the tree. Both of them gasped at what they found.

"Kamal?"

Crouched behind the oak, looking up at them, was Kamal—the elite sapphire mage who'd been killed by the Pishacha. Yuki had forgotten how tall he was until he stood. She continued to stare in wonder as he shook his stringy, black hair out of his face. The kitsune purred and slunk around Kamal's leg.

"I don't know what's more shocking," Mayhara said. "The fact that kitsune exist or that you're standing here before us."

For a second, they simply stared at each other, and then they all let out a relieved laugh and exchanged hugs.

"How…?" Yuki shook her head. "Are you alive?"

Kamal let out a laugh. "I think you know the answer to that. We are in the spirit realm, after all. And weren't you there when I was buried?"

Yuki rubbed the back of her neck. "Yeah. Right."

Kamal eyed them. "So what happened? How did you die?"

"Oh." Mayhara shook her head. "No, we're not dead. We sort of landed here by mistake. A magic mishap. We're actually being chased by one of the dark mages."

Kamal clicked his tongue. "You just can't stay out of trouble, can you?"

Above them, the sky began to change. The comet went from black to silver, its light almost as bright as the moon.

"Oh good," Kamal said. "Our magic's coming back."

"What?" Yuki gawked at him. "Because the sun set?"

"No, it's not as simple as that." Kamal pointed to their wrists. "Our wristbands are lighting up. It comes and goes, day and night. There's no rhyme or reason to it. But what I do know is that when my powers come back, I can finally talk to this guy again." He reached down and pet the kitsune's head.

"He talks?" Yuki asked, astonished.

"Well, no. But my powers somehow let me hear him. Or his thoughts. I don't know exactly. But we can communicate." Kamal picked up the satchel from the ground and stood. "What's this?"

"That's… important," Mayhara answered, but Kamal had already removed the small scroll from the bag.

"Hey, if it's not food, how important can it be?" He smirked and replaced the scroll.

"Wait." Yuki shook her head. "You eat after you're

dead?"

Kamal smirked. "We don't have to, but why should I give up my favorite pastime?"

"The scroll," Mayhara said, getting back to the vital topic. "It supposedly contains a spell that could destroy Kashmeru." She checked over her shoulder. "Which is one of the reasons the dark mage is after us."

"It's so small," Kamal remarked, balancing the scroll in one hand. "I can't imagine it's a long and difficult spell."

"Well, we don't know, to be honest." Yuki shrugged. "Karina couldn't get it open. None of us could."

"There must be some special witchy way to unroll it," Mayhara added.

"Hmm." Kamal handed Yuki the satchel. "You know who you should ask? Amalia."

Mayhara frowned. "Amalia is… dead. The poison finally took her life."

To their surprise, Kamal let out a laugh.

"Yeah, I know," he said. "She's here. Come on. I'll bring you to her."

Eleven

"She's here?" Mayhara asked, flustered. "You've seen her?" There was a tingling warmth in her chest at the prospect.

"Sure," Kamal answered. "We've hung out. You know, discussing philosophy and stuff."

"Why am I having a hard time imagining that?" Yuki

mumbled.

"Have you seen anyone else?" Mayhara asked.

"Here and there." Kamal narrowed his eyes. "You don't know, do you?"

Mayhara shook her head. Yuki looked as if she were going to say something, but then she closed her mouth and waited for Kamal to continue.

"We're all stuck here." He began to walk and waved for them to follow. "Come on. I'll explain on the way."

He led them through a forest, one so different from any Mayhara had ever seen before. The plush carpet of grass beneath their feet glistened in the light of the comet. Every tree seemed to bear some kind of fruit or flower, some of them glowing. The trunks of the trees looked like white stone, structured in a spiral design. She assumed the small floating lights fluttering around were fireflies, but she couldn't be sure. The kitsune bounded along, sometimes darting up ahead and then scurrying back to walk beside Kamal.

"As I was saying," Kamal continued. "This is sort of a holding place, and we're all trapped here. For now, anyway."

"Who's 'we'?" Mayhara struggled to keep up with the

long-legged mage.

"Everyone who's died because of the war with Kashmeru. Amalia says it's not our final destination. That there's a much better place for us, and that we'll get unstuck once the war ends."

"You mean once Kashmeru is destroyed?" Yuki asked.

"Or, you know." Kamal cleared his throat. "The other outcome."

Mayhara felt as if acid were bubbling in her stomach, eating her insides. "If Kashmeru destroys the world and reigns over a new dimension, what happens then? A place worse than this?"

Kamal spared her a glance and let out a sigh as he shrugged. "Either way, we're stuck here until this unfinished business gets resolved." He reached out and plucked a glowing plum from a tree. There was a loud crunch as he bit into it.

As they continued on their way, Mayhara thought about everyone who'd lost their lives as a result of the battle against the Pishacha. Huojin, the elite golden mage who'd been killed by Avi. Riya, Mayhara's colleague and friend who'd been killed because the Pishacha had thought Riya was Mayhara.

97

Yuki's parents.

She didn't want to bring them up, just in case. But it would be good if Yuki could get a chance to see them before they got back to their world.

Assuming they'd be able to get back.

The trees thinned, and they came upon a clearing. Mayhara spotted a small, stone cottage up ahead, marked by a torch affixed like a sconce by the door.

"Is that where Amalia is?" she asked.

"That's her place here, yeah." Kamal whistled, and the kitsune ran up ahead. He gave Mayhara a wink. "He's letting her know company's coming."

Mayhara felt as if they couldn't get there quickly enough. Not that she wasn't appreciative of being able to see Kamal, but knowing Amalia was here and that she might be able to help them with the scroll gave Mayhara a boost of hope.

A maple-scented smoke wafted from the chimney. The house looked like something out of a fairy tale. The kitsune had jumped into an open window, and half a minute later, the front door opened. Mayhara was surprised when a muscular, middle-aged man stepped out. She slowed her pace, furrowing her brow.

"I thought this was Amalia's place," she said.

"It is." Kamal closed the distance between himself and the man, delivering a high-five that made Mayhara blink in confusion. "This is Aiguo. He was Mr. Kitaro's bodyguard. Struck down by the Pishacha while protecting him."

Mayhara and Yuki bowed to him. He placed his feet together swiftly and returned the bow.

"Nice to meet you," Yuki said sweetly. "Are you Amalia's bodyguard now?"

Aiguo smiled. "No. Nothing to guard her from here. I'm merely her companion as we wait for the war to be resolved. Please, come in."

There was a warm glow filling the tiny house. Mayhara and Yuki exchanged glances. She was sure they were thinking the same thing: This felt like a dream.

Crouched over the fireplace, Amalia stoked the fire. She let out a grunt and a sigh as she stood and wiped her hands on her skirt.

"Amalia!" Yuki ran over to her and enveloped her in her arms.

Mayhara had tears in her eyes as she joined their hug, resting her forehead on Amalia's scraggly, gray hair. "This is incredible."

"Yes, yes. It's all very magical. Now, please, give an old woman some room."

They all took a step back, and Mayhara studied the swamp witch.

"Well, have a seat." Amalia gestured to two small couches in the tiny room. "It's a bit snug, but you can rest your haunches a bit before you continue on your journey."

"You know about our journey?" Yuki asked.

"Yes. I've been expecting you." Amalia gave her a wink.

Mayhara crinkled her brow and looked Kamal's way. He simply shrugged in response.

"You knew we were coming?" Yuki asked.

Amalia worked her way onto one of the couches. "My ancestors speak to me all the time, now that I'm here. Their voices are much clearer in the spirit realm. To be honest, sometimes I wish I could switch them off." She let out a low chuckle.

"And they told you we were here?" Mayhara was trying to wrap her mind around the information.

"Actually, they told me the scroll was coming my way. But I figured it had to be one of you bringing it to me."

Amalia's expression darkened. "But first, tell me, how is Karina?"

Mayhara and Yuki exchanged a glance.

"Last we saw her," Mayhara said, "she was fighting off the enemy, protecting the scroll. And us."

"It was her magic—mixed with mine, I guess—that sent us here," Yuki added.

Amalia nodded slowly. "Yes. She may not have known it, but she was sending the scroll to someone who could help. And I'm assuming that since she's not here, she must still be alive."

This insight gave Mayhara hope. She had to assume Penny and the others were still alive as well.

Kamal cleared his throat. "Sorry to interrupt, but is there some kind of messenger or delivery reward for bringing them here?"

Amalia frowned and gave Aiguo a nod. Aiguo retrieved a jar from the counter in what Mayhara assumed was the kitchen and handed it to Kamal.

"Ooh, yeah," Kamal exclaimed. "I love these berries." He tossed one to the kitsune, who caught it in his mouth midair.

"So let's see it." Amalia held her hand out.

"Oh, right." Yuki handed her the satchel.

Amalia smiled. "This is Karina's bag."

"Yes," Yuki replied.

Amalia slowly smoothed her hand over the satchel before opening it and pulling out the scroll.

Mayhara had expected her to perform some kind of spell or recite an incantation, but all she did was flip the gold latch, and the scroll opened.

"How did you—?" Yuki's jaw hung open.

Amalia shrugged. "Maybe I've got the magic of centuries of witches on my side." She turned her attention to the words on the scroll. "Aha. Okay."

"We could leave it open," Yuki suggested to Mayhara. "So Karina doesn't have to worry about opening it when we get back."

Amalia looked up from the scroll. "I doubt it works that way. I have a feeling you two are going to have to learn the spell."

"But we're not witches," Mayhara said.

"Mages are not far off from witches. Perhaps a bit more limited in power." She winked at Kamal this time, and he rolled his eyes in response. "But you can learn the words, memorize them, and recite them to Karina at the tomb. It might work. It *has to* work. I see no other choice."

Mayhara almost said something about not knowing where Karina might be, or if they'd even make it back and find the tomb in time, but she decided to concentrate on thinking positive.

Amalia cleared her throat, holding the scroll up, and began reading out loud.

"Abire hostem
Hoc planum es ex agro
Cum enim venenum componere
boni a Chakras
Abire hostem
Vos ultra
Per virtute divina
demoliti sunt egressi vobiscum
et non est amplius."

Mayhara tried to push down the doubt that they could learn the spell. She could barely get the first words out correctly. But the world depended on this. This would be the most important thing she could ever need to learn.

Hours later, the words of the spell swirled in

Mayhara's mind. Amalia had made them repeat the incantation over and over until they got it right. It wasn't until the sun peeked its rays through the windows that Amalia finally stood and rolled up the scroll.

Even though Mayhara knew the words by heart now, seeing the scroll closed again made her cringe with worry. She hoped that between the two of them, she and Yuki would remember the spell when the time came to use it.

Aiguo escorted them to the door.

"You know where to go?" Amalia asked them.

Yuki nodded. "Yes, I do. I don't know how I do, but I do."

"Sounds perfectly logical to me." Amalia gave them hugs. "Oh. Your wristbands."

Mayhara twisted her hand and noticed her garnet stone glowing. The light had faded during the night, but now it returned. She smiled, knowing her powers would work for a while. She was unaware of what terrain they might need to cross, but she was sure her crimson mage powers would come in handy.

Amalia patted her shoulder. "You have to go. That dark mage is on his way."

"How did you—?" Yuki gaped at her. "We didn't even

tell you about him."

"Amalia tapped her temple with a finger. "Ancestors."

They nodded in unison.

"Right," Mayhara said. "And if our powers are working, that means his probably are, too."

"Then we'd better hurry," Yuki added.

"There's power in numbers." Kamal was suddenly beside them. "The least I can do for my part in this war is accompany you to your destination."

"Thanks, Kamal." Mayhara placed a hand on his shoulder. "We'd be honored."

"Will you be all right, Amalia?" Yuki asked.

"Child, I'm already dead. What more could happen to me?"

Yuki let out an awkward laugh. "I guess you're right."

"Good luck," Aiguo said. "And please tell Mr. Kitaro it was a privilege working with him."

"And give Karina a big hug from me," Amalia added.

"We will." Mayhara waved as they backed away from the house. "Thank you, Amalia."

Twelve

Penny blinked as the spoon she held tapped against the side of a teacup. Everything around her began to come into view, as if she were waking from a dream. She sat at a table in a café. From all around her, the sound of cats meowing filled her ears. A little girl giggled, stroking the back of a fluffy Persian feline as her mother gossiped with a friend over tea and Japanese cheesecake.

She blinked again.

How did I get here?

There was a dull ache in her head, and her body felt as if she'd recently run a marathon. She swallowed hard, trying to remember how she'd ended up in a cat café.

As she shifted in her chair, a sharp pain in her shoulder made her wince. She moved her blouse away from her body a few inches and glanced down to find a bandage taped to her skin.

What happened to me?

Her heart sped up and her breaths grew heavier, but she forced herself to appear calm as she tried to clear her mind so she could think. She didn't want to draw attention to herself, and she didn't need anyone calling the Imperial Police about a crazy person freaking out in a cat café.

What's the last thing I can remember?

Try as she might, she couldn't get a clear image of anything she had recently done. Or seen. Or said. It was as if something was blocking her visions, her memories.

Checking to make sure no one was watching her, she

set down the spoon and stood from the table. Finding no money on her, she decided to simply slip out of the café, hopefully unnoticed. She bit the inside of her cheek as she made her way toward the door. Maybe she would recognize what city she was in once she stepped outside.

The ache in her head subsided a bit as the fresh air out in the street washed over her face. A chill traveled up her spine as she took in her surroundings. Nothing on the street looked familiar at all.

After checking herself for her Linq and coming up emptyhanded, she turned to the menu displayed in the cat café's window.

Ajeetgarh. What am I doing here?

Tears threatened to spill as she realized the direness of her situation. If only she had an idea of whom to contact for help.

Darshana.

Her brow creased. She wasn't even sure if the old guru was still alive. It had been years since she'd last seen her.

Hadn't it?

She wrapped her arms around herself and started walking, unsure of where she should go. The sounds of people talking reached her ears, and she felt a strange pang in her chest at the words 'comet' and 'temple.'

Continuing down the street, the flicker of televiewers displayed in the window of an electronics shop caught her attention. Though she couldn't hear the sound from the screens, she focused on the images of the Lotus Temple displayed on the televiewers.

She didn't know why, but she was overcome with a sense of urgency. Something told her she was supposed to be there.

An Imperial Police van passed her on the street. Instinctively, she turned her head away from it. She could remember always steering clear of the police, but somehow the feeling to hide from them felt even more imperative.

What's happening? And why can't I remember?

Running her hand up her arm to stop from shivering, she scraped against a sensitive spot near her elbow. Hissing in a breath, she would have sworn she heard a voice echo in her head.

Remember.

She froze in place. There was something familiar about the voice, but she couldn't put a name or face to it. Something must have happened that had caused her memories to disappear. Not all of them, but whatever might have happened recently. And someone had known this was going to happen but wanted her to remember.

But how?

Her mind swirled, and her stomach churned. With every panicked breath, she winced at the throbbing ache in her shoulder. Had she been stabbed? Shot? Who would have done this to her? Had it been the police? But then, how had she gotten away and ended up bandaged in a cat café?

There were too many unanswerable questions, and she wasn't sure how she was going to solve the mystery. The only thing she felt certain of was that she needed to get to the Lotus Temple. And soon.

Swallowing back her fear, she picked up her pace. She didn't know how she was going to do it, but she was determined to get to that temple and get some answers, no matter what it took.

Thirteen

Shiro rolled up his sleeping bag and set it near one of the walls of the tent. He'd had a restless sleep, and though he would have benefited from dozing for a while longer, the sounds of the travelers beginning their day—along with the smell of something delectable cooking over a fire—gave him the needed push to get up.

Jae and Mr. Kitaro hadn't woken him when they'd gotten up. Their things were already sitting by the front of the tent, ready to go. He hoped he wasn't holding up the group from leaving. It was an important day. The *most* important day.

He gathered his bags and set them by the others, and then he let out a long breath. He'd been anxious to check his Linq, but he didn't want to face disappointment again. He'd sent a message to Qiang as soon as he'd heard about the prison camp explosions. And when the extremists had been blamed for the attacks, he'd linqed him again. But so far, he hadn't heard back. To make things worse, he'd overheard Jae telling Darshana that some arrests of extremists had already been made. To say he was worried was an understatement.

When he stepped out of the tent, Loni waved him over. The rest of the gang was gathered around Jae's Linq. As he got closer, he realized they were watching a news report.

"...has come forward with evidence that officially links the attacks to the extremists. Governor Laghari has reported that's he's received messages from the extremist leader threatening more attacks. For fear the festival at the Lotus

temple this evening could be a target, acting Police Chief Kang has issued a nationwide decree, allowing Imperial Police to use brute force if any mage is found within a fifty-kilometer radius of the temple. He went as far as to say that the situation has become so extreme, if necessary, police will be permitted to shoot on sight."

Salina gasped, and Shiro rubbed his temples. He couldn't believe it had come to this.

"This is going to make it even more difficult to get to the temple," Loni said.

"They're really going to tighten security now." Jae tucked his Linq into his pocket. "We'll need to get there sooner rather than later, before it's completely locked down."

"I agree." Darshana gave them a curt nod. "We need to go."

Mr. Kitaro cleared his throat. "On that subject, there's something I need to say."

The group turned to face him.

Darshana's brows drew together. "What is it?"

"I don't believe I'm supposed to partake in this leg of the journey."

Salina stared at him, her hands coming up to her mouth.

"I would just get in the way," he continued. "And this mission is too important for you to have to worry about a third wheel… or sixth, as the case may be. I've spoken with Patrin, and he's agreed to let me stay here. For now, I mean. It's safer for you—and for me."

Darshana reached out and took his hand. "My dear Mr. Kitaro."

"If all goes well—"

"*When* all goes well. We have to think positive now."

He smiled at her. "*When* all goes well, you know where to find me."

She lifted his hand and placed a kiss upon it. "We'll come back for you, as soon as we've won the war."

Patrin and Vano approached.

Darshana turned to face them and gave them a bow. "Patrin, I owe you heartfelt thanks. You've been more than hospitable."

"It's nothing compared to what you're doing for us, Darshana." He pulled her in for a hug. "May luck be on your side."

"Salina." Vano closed the distance between them. "I

want you to have this. For luck."

Her eyes widened as he placed a gold chain with a stone pendant in her hand. "I can't take this."

"Think of it as a loan. You can return it to me... after."

She smiled up at him. "Thank you. I will."

Shiro, Jae, and Loni added their thanks, and Patrin had some of the travelers help them with their bags. Shiro felt as if he were having an out-of-body experience as they loaded up the car. He couldn't believe the day of reckoning had finally come. Was he ready for this? Were any of them?

Jae clapped him on the back. "All set?"

Shiro returned the clap. "Now or never, right?"

Before his hand even touched the car door handle, his Linq buzzed. When he looked at the screen, he was surprised to see it wasn't just a return message; Qiang was calling him.

His finger almost slipped when he went to answer it. "Qiang?"

"Shiro." He sounded out of breath.

"I heard about the prison camps. I was worried about you. I mean, I still am."

"I'm okay. I'm glad to hear your voice. I'm lying low. And I'm pissed that we couldn't dismantle all the bombs."

"Don't blame yourself. The Pishacha are the bad guys here." Shiro could remember a time Qiang had said the same thing to him. "Qiang, the police have been instructed to use brute force if they find any mages near the temple."

Qiang sighed into the Linq. "I heard."

"That's why it kills me to have to ask you this."

"What is it?"

Shiro ran a hand through his hair. "If you do this, if we pull this off and stop Kashmeru, we're still going to have his followers to deal with. The police, the government… basically everyone who's going to be at the temple tonight. There's going to be chaos, and we're going to need help containing it."

"Say no more. We'll be there."

"Are you far from New Delhi?"

Qiang let a small laugh escape his lips. "Don't worry. We'll make do. And if it comes to it, I think I know a place where I can borrow a helicopter."

Shiro almost laughed, but something told him Qiang wasn't kidding.

Fourteen

They'd stopped by a stream and cupped their hands in the water to drink from it. Yuki had used the time when their powers had been working to keep Mayhara's mood—as well as her own—elevated. It wouldn't do to have them lose hope. But the haze reappeared around the sun, the comet turned black again, and their wristbands were no longer lit up. She hoped the couple of hours of mood-boosting had been enough to keep their spirits lifted until their powers came back into effect.

The kitsune jumped into the stream to drink, and then it rolled around in the water. When it strolled out onto the bank, it shook its body and all nine tails, practically soaking Kamal.

"Kamal, does he have a name?" Yuki asked, taking the opportunity of their short break to sit and rub her aching feet.

"Akari."

"That's cute," Mayhara said.

"It means 'bright, white jasmine.' But believe me, you spend time with him after he's had a few too many cabbages, and it's not flowers he smells like."

Akari chittered at him.

"How much farther is it, do you think, Yuki?" Mayhara flattened her hand over her eyes, looking out into the distance. "I can't help feeling we're cutting it close."

Yuki put her shoes back on and stood. "We're almost there."

Mayhara's eyes went to Kamal. "Do you know where

we're headed?"

Kamal wiped drops of water from his cheek. "I'm not the spirit realm mage. The ball's in Yuki's court."

Mayhara shrugged. "I just thought because you've been here, you might have an idea of what awaits us in the direction we're headed."

"That way?" Kamal stretched his back and his neck, narrowing his eyes. "There are some caves that way."

"Yes." Yuki clapped her hands together and held her index fingers to her mouth. "That sounds right. Something was telling me I needed to find a cave."

"Okay, then." Mayhara wiped her hands on her jeans. "Let's go."

It was another hour before they could even catch a glimpse of the caves. They were nestled in the side of a hill, and farther out, the hill became a mountain.

Yuki picked up her pace, excited to finally be getting to their destination. The fog was low and covered any sight of the ground, so when her feet began to sink into what felt like sand, she let out a gasp of surprise.

"Oh, it's sand." She held out her hands to regain her balance.

From behind her, Kamal called out. "Yuki, stop!"

"What?" Mayhara froze beside him. "What is it?"

"It's quicksand!" Kamal took careful steps, his arms reaching for Yuki, but she was too far in.

Yuki scoffed. "You didn't think to mention the quicksand earlier? Don't you think that would have been an important detail to warn us about?"

"I forgot about it! Sorry!" Kamal crouched down and stretched his arm toward her, but it was of no use.

Yuki shifted her weight, trying to keep her legs from sinking deeper into the sand.

Akari let out sounds between barks and wails, running back and forth behind Kamal, probably knowing he was unable to help.

"Stop struggling," Mayhara called. "It'll only make you sink faster."

"I'm just supposed to *not* move?"

"If you die here, you'll be stuck like the rest of us. You won't be able to leave. I'll see if I can find a branch or something." Kamal ran off toward a patch of bushes.

Mayhara paced, looking up at the sun. Yuki followed her gaze. The sparkling haze went from blue to pink.

"Come on," Mayhara mumbled.

Yuki couldn't find her breath, starting to feel

suffocated. She wanted to lift her legs, but that would go against Mayhara's advice.

"How's it going, Kamal?" Yuki forced her voice to remain as calm as she could manage.

Kamal ran back with a flimsy branch. "Grab hold."

Yuki wrapped her hands around the thin branch, ignoring the sting in her palm from something sharp. Kamal pulled gently, not wanting to break the branch. Mayhara wrung her hands, constantly checking the sun.

The thick, wet sand clung to Yuki's legs, which now felt as if they were made of lead.

"Don't let go," Kamal urged.

"I don't think it's working," Yuki exclaimed.

"Okay, it's happening!" Mayhara suddenly shouted.

Yuki looked up. The sparkling haze around the sun disappeared. The diamond on her wristband glowed a bright white.

Mayhara held her palms out, facing Yuki. The red glow in her palms expanded. Yuki felt her feet make contact with something hard, like rock. The rock pushed upward, lifting her. The sand at her sides hardened, creating a solid surface. She placed her hands upon it and used it as leverage to pull herself out of the sand trap.

Kamal grabbed her arms and pulled her the rest of the way out.

"Okay, I don't know how long this is going to last," Mayhara said, her palms out and still glowing red. "I'm going to hold it solid as long as I can, and I say we make a run for it."

Yuki's legs were still covered in the drying wet sand, but she nodded. "Agreed. Let's go."

She had to trust that Mayhara had control over the surface and that the haze would be gone long enough for them to make their trek to the caves. She didn't want to be stuck like that ever again. Pushing down thoughts about how the lack of air to her lungs was making her chest hurt, or how heavy her legs felt with caked-on mud clinging to her, she continued to pump her legs. It helped that Akari was darting out in front of them, hightailing it, as it were, toward the caves. As long as she could concentrate on him bounding across the surface, she knew it was still safe for her to run.

At long last, and without a breath to spare, they crossed over onto a grassy knoll that stood before the caves.

"We made it," Kamal said once he could breathe

again.

Mayhara looked up at the sky. "The haze is till gone. The comet's white. We should still have our powers."

"Good," Yuki said. "Because the caves look like they're blocked."

Mayhara pushed her hair away from her sweaty face to see that the entrance of the caves were indeed blocked by piles of rock and boulders. "Of course they are. Which cave do we need?"

Yuki pointed, constantly checking the sun and the comet.

Mayhara held her palm out toward the cave she'd indicated. Crimson particles traveled from her hand to the boulders blocking the cave entrance. One crack. Two. And then suddenly the whole blockage crumbled before their eyes. A heap of dirt stood at the foot of the cave entrance, dust flying off in the air. Akari was the first to hop the dirt pile and run inside.

No one spoke as they entered. They used the glow of their hands to light the way. Akari was particularly useful, his white fur reflecting the light, helping them to better see in the dark.

The entrance tunnel led to an open cavern, its walls lit

up by thousands of tiny glowing crystals. Yuki skidded to a stop as two figures appeared to one side of the cavern. Her breath got stuck in her throat when she realized they were her parents, smiling back at her.

"Mama? Papa?" Her heart felt like mush. Tears flowed down her cheeks as she ran to them. "I was afraid to believe I'd see you here."

Her parents pulled her closer, snuggling her in their arms.

"Our darling," her mother said. "You've grown so much."

Yuki reveled in the feel of her mother's breath on her hair. "I'm so sorry," she said as she pulled back to look at them.

"No, dear," her father said. "You have nothing to be sorry about. You are fulfilling your destiny."

"But I didn't mean for you to die."

"You were not the one who killed us," her mother said, gently pushing back a strand of Yuki's hair. "You are not to blame. Please remember that."

Yuki hugged them again, bawling. She was barely aware that Mayhara and Kamal were patiently watching them.

"It's time for you to go," her father said, stroking her cheek.

"Already?"

Her mother pressed her forehead against Yuki's. "I'm afraid so, darling. We love you. Don't ever forget that."

Yuki kissed both their cheeks, hating that she had to let them go. She reluctantly backed away from them until she felt Mayhara's hand on her shoulder.

"Where to now?" Mayhara asked.

Yuki wiped the tears from her eyes. She turned and surveilled the cavern. It was riddled with stalagmites and stalactites. At the far end was a tunnel.

"That way," she said, leading them in that direction. She forced herself not to turn around to look at her parents. She knew, if she did, she'd never want to leave.

Mayhara and Kamal were right behind her. Though she couldn't see where Akari was, she could hear his chittering.

The tunnel forked off into two directions, but Yuki somehow knew where to go. The other two mages followed her without question. At the end of the tunnel stood large, wooden, double doors.

"This looks familiar," Mayhara said.

Yuki tried pulling on one of the cast-iron handles. "It's heavy."

Kamal snaked his hand through the handle beside Yuki's and yanked. When they managed to pull it open a crack, Mayhara grabbed the edge of the door, grunting as she helped force it open.

Suddenly, the door swung open wider, and Yuki almost screamed when she discovered two young women pushing the door from the other side.

One of them had long, black hair and glimmering, green eyes. Yuki couldn't help but think she looked like Loni. The other had even straighter black hair, which fell like a curtain of silk to her shoulders. She had big eyes and high cheekbones.

"Huojin?" Mayhara's lips curled into a smile.

The young woman she'd spoken to gave her a shy grin before Mayhara embraced her.

Mayhara tuned to Yuki and Kamal. "This is Huojin. She was the elite golden mage before Salina."

Kamal gave her a cocky, sideways smirk. "I know who she is. And this is Kanya. She's Loni's sister."

"Sorry we have to cut the reunion short," Huojin put in, "but you don't have much time. The dark mage is approaching."

"And if we wait any longer, your powers won't work." Kanya took Yuki and Mayhara by their upper arms and urged them to come farther into the room.

Only it wasn't a room; it was another cavern. But this one had an extremely high ceiling and it contained an enormous structure in its center. It was almost like a towering statue made up of seven orbs of light, connected by rock and crystal swirling in a vertical column that went from the cavern floor to its ceiling. If Yuki had to guess, she'd say it was about ten feet in diameter. She couldn't even guess how high it was.

The orbs contained moving, glowing particles. The bottom orb's particles were deep red. Above it, sparkling orange. Those were followed with spheres of yellow, then green, then blue, then purple, and finally, at the top, a brilliant white.

"It's the mage colors," Yuki said as she stared at the structure in awe.

"The same colors as the chakras," Mayhara added. "I've seen this before, at the academy. Jae showed it to me, except the spheres weren't glowing. The lights were all out.

"This is your way back," Huojin said. "You two represent both ends of the spiral. Mayhara at the base, Yuki at the top."

Kanya eyed the structure. "You need to use your powers to move the particles at each end, get the particles moving faster, until the whole thing lights up."

"It *is* lit up," Mayhara insisted.

"Oh." Huojin laughed. "That's not lit up. You wait and see."

"Think of it as unblocking the chakras." Kanya glanced toward the door. "But you have to start now. We'll hold off the dark mage as long as we can."

Yuki swallowed hard. "He's here?"

"Don't worry, he can't hurt us," Huojin said. "We're already dead. But we need to keep him away, to stop him from stopping you."

As soon as she'd finished her sentence, the wooden door creaked.

"Do it, Mayhara!" Huojin yelled. Her arms were already raised and her palms aimed at the door.

A screech echoed in the cavern as the door swung open. Avi stood in the doorway, his eyes scanning the cavern and the people within in. His shirt was now completely bloody. His eyes dropped as he stumbled into the space.

Kanya's palms glowed green, and Huojin's emanated golden light. When they pushed out their energy, a swirling shield of air and fire hovered in front of them.

Avi's brow furrowed, and Yuki wondered if he hadn't yet figured out that his powers depended on the cycle of the sparkling haze.

Huojin snarled at him. "It's payback time, you jerk."

Avi bared his teeth. He lifted his hand, and black particles flew out in a stream through the air, hitting the fire shield. Most of the particles ricocheted off the shield, but Yuki was shocked to see some of the particles breaking through.

"A little help, Kamal!" Kanya shouted.

Kamal had already been beside them, but now he used his sapphire mage powers to blast Avi back with soundwaves.

Yuki and Mayhara exchanged a glance. Without another word, they held their hands out, palms facing the structure. Yuki held hers higher, aiming her diamond energy at the top sphere. Mayhara's particles were already lighting up the red orb. Huojin was right: the spheres lit up into practically blinding, bright lights.

"He's getting through!" Kanya yelled.

Yuki snuck a glance over her shoulder. She spotted Akari in a pouncing position just before he charged Avi and knocked him down, all nine tails swaying as he swung around and bounded back to Kamal's side.

"Yuki, concentrate!" Mayhara already had the red and orange spheres fully lit.

Yuki snapped back to the task at hand and pushed out her energy harder. She had to trust that the three spirits of mages—and the kitsune—could hold off Avi.

Come on, Yuki. Everyone's counting on you.

The white sphere was now completely lit, and the purple one was getting brighter. It was exhausting, but she wouldn't let up. Mayhara had half the green sphere glowing brightly and gaining ground fast.

Yuki let out a long groan as she reached deep down inside of herself and pushed out as much energy as she could. Now, she only had to finish lighting up the blue sphere.

"Mayhara!" Huojin yelled. "Tell Loni I'm sorry!"

"Hug my sister for me!" Kanya shouted.

The lights became so bright that Yuki could only see

white. She wasn't sure if the vibrating hum in her ears was coming from the structure or from Kamal's magic. It all became so intense, she was sure her head would explode.

And then suddenly there was a pop, and everything fell silent. She felt her stomach drop, and nausea overwhelmed her. Her head spun, and she feared she would fall over. The bright, white light slowly faded to black.

She blinked, spots dancing in her eyes.

"Mayhara?"

At first, there was no answer. And then...

"I'm right here." Mayhara's voice sounded weak.

The surroundings slowly came into focus. The structure with the spheres stood before her, but nothing was lit up. Everything was dark.

Yuki glanced around. The other mages—the spirits—were nowhere to be seen. She turned and focused on Mayhara, who appeared frazzled and frightened. "Are we back?"

"I think so," Mayhara said. "And I feel like I'm going to throw up."

Yuki grabbed Mayhara by the wrists. "We did it?"

Mayhara stared at her, the color slowly returning to

her face. Yuki released her wrists so Mayhara could scrub her hands down her face. Yuki held her breath in anticipation.

"Okay, I'm ready. Let's go check." Mayhara took her hand and led the way.

They had to climb stone steps to reach the wooden doors, and Yuki realized they couldn't have been in the same cavern they'd been in before. The spheres had served as a portal from the spirit world.

Once they were out of the cavern and running through a hallway, Yuki began to recognize that they were in the demolished academy. The walls were rubble, and the place was covered in dirt and dust. She couldn't remember it looking so battered and broken. Though her heart wept for the place, an energy of hope ran through her.

"We're back," Mayhara whispered. "We're home."

Yuki's heart hammered in her chest. "What now?"

"Now we get to New Delhi."

Fifteen

Naree sat comfortably in the back of the limousine. She used breathing exercises to remain calm. Today was the day. By night's end, she would finally be reunited with her true love.

My darling, I can feel your anticipation. I, too, am overjoyed that we will soon be together.

Naree closed her eyes, reveling in Kashmeru's voice. She wanted to answer him, but a set of eyes were locked on her.

Karina sat across from her, watching her. For a moment, Naree suspected the witch might be able to hear Kashmeru's voice as well. She tilted her head and narrowed her eyes at her, wondering what she might say.

"You don't have to do this, you know?" Karina glanced over her shoulder, most likely wondering if the driver could hear her.

Our time has come at last, my love. Don't let the witch dissuade you.

"This is destiny," Naree said to Karina. Though she meant for Kashmeru to hear it as well. "Centuries in the making."

"This is a trick," Karina protested. "He's using you. That's what evil does. Why would someone who loves you make you turn against your own army?"

I have a new army for you, my love. A better, stronger army. More powerful than you can imagine. All for you.

"It is but a small sacrifice compared to what he's promised me." Naree opened her clutch and took out a compact to check her face. When she returned it, her fingers brushed against the smooth jade dragonfly Jae had carved for her. Her brow furrowed; she didn't remember putting it in her purse. Feeling Karina's stare, she snapped the clutch closed and whipped her chin up. "Every sacrifice is worth it. His love for me is all I'll ever need."

There was a pity in Karina's eyes. The sudden change of expression made Naree blanch. She ran her hand gently over her clutch, her mind on the jade dragonfly. Jae loved her too. Her brother's love for her had also filled her with joy. Her mind went to her parents, probably waiting back home for their daughter to finally come home.

What are you doing? Kashmeru's voice was full of rage.

Naree flinched. Karina shot her a questioning look.

Do not be led astray. Tonight, everything changes. No one can stop us. Or do you need a reminder of my power?

A sudden, razor-sharp pain bit into Naree's spine. She let out a cry as she arched her back, trying to make the ache stop. It felt like nails made of fire were clawing into her.

Karina sat upright, her eyes wide. "Your Highness? What's wrong?"

Do we understand each other? Or should I continue this torture to convince you?

"No! Please!"

As quickly as it had started, the pain stopped. Karina

swallowed hard, sitting on the edge of her seat and appearing ready to jump to her rescue, even though she was oblivious to what had just happened. Naree tried to control her erratic breaths, shifting in her seat and pushing her hair out of her face.

"Your Highness?"

Naree's lips twisted into a snarl. "Who are you to question me? To assume to be a master of what fate has in store for me? You are nothing. You are here for one reason only, and that is to do my bidding. Anything beyond that is unacceptable."

Karina's mouth fell into a straight line as she backed up in her seat. She averted her gaze, and Naree let out a long, exasperated breath.

You will soon see, my love. It will all be worth it. We will be together, as we should be. And together, we will reign over our new, perfect world.

Penny kept her eye on the roadside. She knew she was getting closer.

"The academy is up ahead," Qiang said from the driver's seat.

"Yep." She turned to face him. "They'll be there. Trust me."

"Oh, don't worry." Qiang gave her a wink. "You're the elite amethyst mage. I trust you completely."

She flashed him a smile. It had only been a few hours since she'd found Qiang. Her visions had begun to return to her after she'd left the café. The voice that followed her had become louder as the morning went on.

Remember.

The voice made her touch a spot on her arm, a spot marked by magic. And then it had all come back to her. Piece by piece. It was Karina's voice bringing her back, restoring her memories bit by bit, until it had all fallen into place.

She'd been possessed by Bhutano, and through her, he'd manipulated the mages and stolen all the daggers. Helplessly watching it all play out through her own eyes was the worst torture she'd ever been through.

If it hadn't been for Karina, Penny would still be possessed by Kashmeru's spirit messenger—or possibly dead from the diamond bullet wound—and her memories would have been forever lost. Luckily, Karina had marked her with a spell that would help her remember everything.

Now, she was herself again, and her visions had led her first to find Qiang. Her visions were now leading her to the academy to find two important elements of the puzzle: Mayhara and Yuki.

"There they are," she called out excitedly, pointing at the two figures traveling along the road on foot.

Qiang picked up speed.

Mayhara's and Yuki's faces became more recognizable as they got closer. Penny's heart leapt with exhilaration and her head swam with relief. Both Mayhara and Yuki froze when they saw her, their jaws hanging open.

Qiang barely stopped the car before Penny jumped out. She almost knocked Mayhara over when she pounced on her for a hug.

Mayhara was a little stiff, and then Penny remembered that the last time they'd seen each other, she'd been possessed by Bhutano.

"Mayhara, it's me. It's Penny. Really."

Mayhara glanced at Yuki, shock still apparent on her face.

Yuki's palms glowed white. "By the gods, it's really

you."

Penny was so thrilled, she let out a laugh as she threw her arms around Yuki.

"What are you—?" Mayhara shook her head, but a smile finally formed on her lips. "How did you find us?"

"Amethyst powers. They led me to Qiang first." She pointed to Qiang in the car, to whom they both waved. "And then to you. I can tell you more on the way. We need to hurry."

Penny signaled for them to follow and climbed back into the car.

"On the way to the temple?" Yuki asked as she buckled in.

"That's the final destination, yeah," Qiang said, swiftly turning the car around once Mayhara had closed her door.

"The other elites should be there," Penny said. "The vision's not clear. But hopefully we can find them and actually pull this thing off."

Qiang sped up the car. "But first, we've got to see if Mitty was able to get me a helicopter."

Sixteen

Scaffolding still stood around part of the flowerlike shape of the Bahá'i Lotus Temple. But the delay in completing the renovation of the building was apparently not going to stop the festival from taking place. The building was comprised of twenty-seven freestanding marble towers called 'petals' that were arranged in clusters of three, forming its nine sides. Nine enormous pools of water surrounded the building, set apart by stone steps and pathways that led to its nine doors. Only, tonight, the organizers of the festival had six of the doors blocked off to better control admission. One of those doors was being used by the event planners, the festival decorators, and the hired caterers.

Because of the enormous lay of land around the temple, the caterer vans were parked in one of the parking lots located about a six-minute walk from the temple. Jae used his sapphire mage powers to convince five of the caterers to go home sick, leaving their uniforms and access badges behind. The mages and Darshana used one of the vans to slip on their white, button-down shirts and maroon serving aprons. There were so many workers that evening, Jae was sure it would be hard for the event planners to keep track.

"Are we ready to do this?" Salina asked. "I can't help but feel we're ill prepared, especially because we're not a complete team."

"We don't have a choice." Jae's gaze traveled between the mages and Darshana. "We can get to the tomb and try to somehow stop the Pishacha with the limited power we've got."

"Maybe the others will show up." Shiro didn't look convinced as he said it.

"We'll do what we can." Darshana let out a slow breath. "It's all we can do."

They pushed two catering carts filled with food to the entrance being used by the waitstaff. Jae forced himself to look like he belonged there, so as not to draw suspicion from the police patrolling the area. He spotted their cyber-batons and their pistols and hoped there wouldn't be a run-in to stop them from finding the tomb. It was still hours before the festival would begin, but the place was already packed. A man dressed in a black suit with a maroon vest and bowtie held up his hand as they approached the door.

"Sorry, I don't recognize any of you." He lifted his electronic tablet and checked the screen. "Your names please?"

Jae checked the area to make sure none of the police who were patrolling the temple were watching. He then pushed out his sapphire energy, his palms glowing a brilliant blue. He hoped the comet's interference wouldn't get in the way of his powers.

"You don't need our names," Jae said. "You are happy to see us and welcome us inside."

The man blinked, and a second later, he smiled. "Glad to see you. Come in and take those carts down to the kitchen. There's a service elevator to the left."

"Perfect," Jae replied. "Thank you."

He led the others past the man, rolling the cart toward the elevator.

"Are we really going to the kitchen?" Salina asked.

"We think the tomb is under the building somewhere," Jae replied. "The kitchen is already at a lower level. I'm sure we can find access to wherever the tomb might be located down there."

There was a ding as the elevator doors opened. Two Imperial Police officers stood inside. Salina stiffened, and Loni turned her head so her hair covered her face. Darshana and Jae remained facing forward, and Shiro dropped his chin, pretending to adjust his apron strings.

Jae's white-knuckle grip on the catering cart remained tight and tense until the police exited the elevators and passed them.

Salina let out a breath of relief as they rolled the carts into the elevator.

"We're not in the clear yet," Jae whispered. "Don't look directly into the camera in the upper corner. There will probably also be cameras in the kitchen, so try not to be obvious."

His words must have jolted them, because they were silent during the ride down.

The elevator announced they'd arrived at sub-level two. Jae was trying to calculate in his head how much farther they might have to go to find the tomb. When the door opened, they rolled out the carts.

Jae led them to where the other carts were parked, and then he subtly made his way through the enormous kitchen. When one of the cooks looked their way, he noticed Shiro's palm glowing orange, and the water in the pot next to the cook began bubbling over. The cook diverted his attention to the pot and forgot about their group.

Jae checked over his shoulder to make sure the rest of the gang was following him. He spotted a door marking the stairwell. He used his powers to silence any alarm that might sound as he pushed the bar to open the door. Glad when the group was ushered through without incident, he turned to check the stairwell.

They took one flight down until they came to a door and a dead end. The door was marked with a yellow triangle sporting a black lightning bolt symbol. There was no handle. To the right of the door was a lock pad.

"Allow me," Salina said, coming forward. "When the system overrides, we'll only have a few seconds to get through, so everyone get ready." She placed her hand on the lock pad. Her palms glowed gold. In the next moment, the lock pad light went out and the door clicked open.

"Go!" she said.

They all darted through the door, almost falling over each other as Salina click the door closed.

They found themselves in some sort of utility hall. Pipes ran along one wall, and the opposite wall was filled with fuse boxes and other electrical control panels.

"Let's see what's at the end of the hall," Jae suggested.

When they got to the end, Jae let out a curse. He was about to turn around when Loni called out, "Wait!"

They all turned to her as she felt the upper and lower parts of the wall.

"I feel air," she said. "There's something on the other side."

"There must be a way to get to the other side of the

wall," Darshana put in. "Or it's more likely some kind of door. Feel the bricks. Maybe one of them acts as a spring release."

Their hands were all over the wall, pushing and pressing. Jae wasn't sure which of them had found the release brick, but the door suddenly swung open.

And beyond the door: darkness.

"You think this is it?" Shiro asked.

Jae pursed his lips. "Only one way to find out."

Naree checked her reflection in the standing mirror. The dress was the purest white and the softest silk. Three thin bands of gold made up the belt that was secured around her waist. The sleeves flowed like air around her arms, and the V-cut neckline accented the gold necklace that clung to her cleavage. Her hair was swept up in a set of gold bands that matched her belt, and a few, soft, loose curls hung freely from the coiffure.

She sucked in a shuddered breath. Was this really happening? Kashmeru was near. She could feel it. Though she'd longed for this moment to come to fruition, part of her questioned if she was really ready to see him.

Lakshmi, it is time.

The door to the chamber opened, and Bhutano stepped in.

"Your Highness, we are ready."

She forced herself to steady her breathing as she followed him into the adjoining room. Six dark mages were lined up, all dressed in black. On a long side table, the seven arcane daggers were set out, each of them sitting on a red, satin cloth. Someone had gone to great lengths to polish them, because they gleamed brilliantly in the light.

Naree ran her fingers along the hilts of each one as she walked by them. They were the key to releasing her true love from the tomb in which he was imprisoned.

Yes, my love. It won't be long now.

She turned to face Bhutano. Behind him, cowering near the wall, was Karina. She had been made to change as well, and the dress she donned was almost as lovely as her own. Karina stood with one arm crossed over her waist, the light blue dress flowing loosely over her form. Someone had brushed the tangles out of her hair.

Naree moved her attention over to the mages. "It's supposed to be the Council of the Seven. We're missing one."

"Your Highness," Bhutano said. "We can only assume that Avi is dead."

"Has anyone informed his father?"

"That won't be necessary. The governor is well aware—as are all of Kashmeru's followers—of the risks that come with being invited to his kingdom. All are willing to sacrifice themselves for the reward."

"And what about the ritual? Will this even work?" A small part of her sparked with hope. Maybe she wouldn't have to go through with this at all. But that small part was quickly pushed down by fear of torture… along with a burning sadness of not being able to see Kashmeru again.

My love. I long to hold you again. I need to see you with my own eyes. Feel you. Come to me.

"I will take Avi's place in the ritual. As Kashmeru's spirit messenger, I'm the only one who can step in for a dark mage."

Naree smoothed her hands over the soft material of her dress. "Very well."

"We must go down to the tomb now, Your Highness.

The comet approaches."

She gave him a nod. The dark mages each took a dagger and placed it the inside pockets of their jackets. Bhutano took the seventh and then gestured for Naree to lead them out of the room.

It is time, my love. Come set me free.

Seventeen

Yuki's heart thrummed in her chest as she and Mayhara followed close behind Penny into the temple. Qiang and Mitty were gathered outside, hiding from the authorities while they assembled the extremists, waiting for the signal to make their move. Penny's palms glowed of amethyst energy, cloaking herself and Yuki and Mayhara from sight. Yuki was amazed when everyone at the party simply looked through them as if they weren't there.

Before they'd entered the building, Penny had instructed them to follow her and not to speak. She'd said she knew exactly where to go, based on visions she'd received.

As they passed through the central hall, Yuki took a moment to admire the festivities. There were thousands of people in attendance. Glittering arches of vines and flowers were spread out in various parts of the room. Paper lanterns were strung across the space. She spotted an elevated koi pond, the center of which contained a lotus-shaped fountain spouting water. Elegant standing tables draped with cream-colored silk tablecloths adorned one section of the room. The centerpieces spilled over with lilies, cherry blossoms, eucalyptus branches, and lavender. Everyone had tall flutes of pink champagne in their hands. Classical music played softly throughout the hall as people conversed.

And no one noticed them walk through it all.

Penny led them down a hall, and eventually they went through a door to a stairwell. Once they were in the clear,

Penny lifted the cloaking energy.

Yuki should have been exhausted. She'd been up for two days, and traveling between two dimensions had literally knocked the wind out of her. Instead, she was filled with a strange exhilaration, a second wind made of both hope and fear. Seeing her parents had given her determination. She just hoped it was enough to defeat Kashmeru.

As they made their way through strange halls and hidden stone steps, they found themselves in an alcove of a large crypt. The ceiling must have been seven meters high. They were hidden from view by statues and tall headstones. In the center of the crypt, a large ray of light shone down onto a sarcophagus.

"Is that it?" Yuki whispered.

"It must be," Mayhara answered.

Penny was narrowing her eyes. "The others are near."

Yuki ducked her head. "You mean the Pishacha?"

"No." Penny pointed across the room.

Yuki spotted the top of someone's head behind a statue of the god Vishnu. She straightened realizing it was Jae. Before she could call out to him, Penny stopped her, holding a finger to her lips.

They traveled along the row of statues, making their way toward the other mages. Yuki was so glad they were all there and unharmed.

Jae's eyes widened as they rounded the corner. Salina slapped her hand over her mouth, and although Shiro seemed thrilled to see them, he let out a warning shush, reminding them that they were there in secret.

They kept their voices low as they ran to hug one another. The first to embrace were Jae and Mayhara. He spun her around as soon as he lifted her into his arms.

Darshana ran a hand over Yuki's hair. "We were so worried about you."

"Mayhara and I were sent to the spirit realm."

"Amalia was there," Mayhara added. "She opened the scroll."

"Where is it?" Loni asked.

"It could only be opened by her," Yuki explained. "But Mayhara and I memorized the spell."

"Karina's not with you?" Shiro asked.

"We got separated. The Pishacha have her. And the daggers," Penny said. "There's so much to tell you, but in the end, Karina made a deal with the Pishacha so they would release me. She promised them she would perform the unbinding spell."

"But we're all here now," Mayhara said. "We can stop them."

"Someone's coming," Penny said, her gaze far away.

"We've got the element of surprise on our side." Jae moved closer to the center of the crypt. "Get ready."

The others followed his lead, taking their stances. Hands lifted, palms facing forward, they were ready to fight.

Eighteen

Karina couldn't slow the pounding in her ears. She was surrounded by dark mages as they made their way to the tomb. In front of her, Naree was mysteriously quiet. In her head, Karina was struggling with her options to get out of this. One thought was to recite the spell incorrectly. Would they believe her if she said it simply hadn't worked? That she'd gotten it wrong? Or would that just anger the dark god, and he'd command the dark mages to kill her?

Weighed against the destruction of the universe, it seemed a sensible sacrifice.

Yes. That was what she would do. Her death would be worth saving the world, wouldn't it?

The crypt was a dark, dank place. The surrounding statues and headstones lurked like shadows of evil spirits, ready to pounce if she made one wrong move.

Suddenly, there was so much movement, she couldn't keep track of what was happening. The dark mages took defensive stances. And in front of them, standing just beyond the sarcophagus in the center of the room, were all seven mages.

They're here! They made it!

She could barely make out Darshana's figure somewhere at the back of the room.

The pounding in her ears intensified. Palms were lit up everywhere, and Karina backed up behind a headstone for fear she'd get caught in the crossfire.

Black particles zipped across the room but were blocked by a sudden crimson shield that materialized between the dark mages and the elite. Fire then roared across the crypt in the shape of a whip, but one of the dark mages—Harish—raised his hand and syphoned the fire from the air. As another dark mage released a swarm of black energy, a harsh wind whipped toward it over the sarcophagus, blowing back the swarm and knocking two dark mages off their feet. A cloud of purple smoke seeped from Penny's palm, blinding their view.

And then Naree let out a guttural scream. Her palms glowed with all the seven chakra colors. She threw out her arms, and the bright prism of colors shot across the crypt in heavy streams that made the elite mages stumble back a few steps.

Karina had to squint to see what had happened. What she saw confused her. The seven elite mages stood frozen, their arms stiff at their sides, their heads held high as if in a vise, and their eyes wide with fright. Their feet were six inches off the ground, their bodies floating from Naree's magic. Their breathing was erratic, but otherwise, they didn't move. They'd been put into some sort of state of paralysis.

Bhutano looked pleased. The dark mages reassembled around the Lotus, smirking at their enemies.

"Your efforts are futile," Naree said, confidence in her voice. She patted her hair back into place. "You cannot stop fate. And now you must watch as Kashmeru wins his victory."

Naree approached the sarcophagus and ran her hands along the top, her fingers moving with the grooves that were carved into the stone. Ru glanced at Karina and squared her jaw. With a hard grip, she took Karina by the arm and yanked her toward the stone coffin.

Naree looked up to the light that was flooding in from the spot in the ceiling. "The comet is at its apex. It's time."

Karina followed her gaze. The light must have been coming through from above. She knew the center of the main hall of the Lotus Temple had a star-shaped window in the roof. She wondered if the window was duplicated in the floor of the hall and every sublevel of the building, all the way down to Kashmeru's tomb. If it hadn't been constructed that way before, there was no doubt the powers in charge had written it into the renovation plans, just for this purpose. The comet's energy flowing through those windows and hitting the sarcophagus was the celestial energy Naree needed to complete the ritual.

"Karina, the spell." Naree's eyes were closed as she

waited. There was even a small smile formed on her face, as if she were enjoying the moment.

Karina let out a shuddered breath. She was ready to die so the binding spell couldn't be undone.

Naree's eyes popped open. "Karina."

She shook her head. "I… I won't."

Naree bared her teeth. "Maybe you haven't noticed, but I have your friends in a very vulnerable position. One snap of my fingers, and they all perish."

Karina's gaze flew to the elite mages. Jae looked like he was trying to shake his head. Tears flowed from Mayhara's eyes. Loni was blinking rapidly, her face contorted like she was in pain. Karina couldn't let them die. She knew it could mean the end of the world, but could she really just let the elite mages perish without doing anything about it? She wasn't about to let them die at her hands. She had no choice but to do the spell.

"O-Okay. Okay. I'll do it." Karina's voice was a whisper.

Naree nodded to the dark mages. They each came forward and stood in a semi-circle around Naree, daggers drawn and held parallel to their chests. Rikuto held a hand out, which Naree took to help hoist herself up onto the top of the sarcophagus. Once she was on top, she kneeled and held her arms out, bathing in the light.

Ru nudged Karina. Karina swallowed back her impending tears and began reciting the spell. All plans to mess up the incantation on purpose went out the window. As she finished the spell the second time, dark tendrils of smoke wafted up from the sarcophagus. The energy in the room felt morose and full of doom.

"The unbinding is complete," Karina said, tears flowing down her cheeks.

She expected Bhutano or one of the dark mages to strike her down, to kill her now that she'd done her part by performing the unbinding spell and was of no use to them anymore. But they didn't seem to pay her any mind. Instead, she was shocked when one of the dark mages— Rikuto—approached Naree and rammed his dagger between two of her ribs. The impact created a burst of black smoke. Naree let out a deafening shriek, her head thrown back and her arms spread at her sides. Blood quickly spread at her side, drenching her white dress and trailing down her body.

Karina gasped. Her eyes went to Jae, who was baring his teeth in frustration, his eyes filled with tears.

DIAMOND *Mage*

A bright red, glittering glow covered Naree's skin. Her eyes were aflame with a harsh, red light. As she screamed, her skin changed from flesh to hard, cracked earth. And then, the ground shook. Rubble and dirt fell from the walls as the shaking intensified. The sound of the earthquake magnified as the floor beneath them began to crack. The shaking was more violent than any earthquake Karina had ever experienced. Her teeth chattered in her head from the vibration, and she had to grab on to the nearest statue to keep her footing. She was sure all of New United Asia was suffering from the quake. It felt like forever until the rumbling stopped. The earth that had been Naree's skin cracked and disintegrated into dust, falling away until Naree's skin was exposed again.

Her blood dripped down her body, leaking into the carvings on the lid of the sarcophagus. Karina believed her blood was dripping through the grooves into the coffin, dousing Kashmeru's corpse.

Naree's breaths were hard and heavy, but there was hardly time for her to recover before the next dark mage—Kun—came forward and drove his dagger into Naree's side. Again, black smoke erupted from the impact. Her scream was louder this time. A copper glow washed over her, orange light shining from her eyes. This time, her body went liquid. It still held its form, but it was like she was made of water. She continued to scream, and water shot from her hands in continuous streams. From all ends of the crypt, water blasted in, flooding the entire room. Ice-cold water poured from the ceiling, drenching everyone. Finally, the water slipped off Naree, leaving her normal body where it should have been, and the water stopped filling the room.

Ru came forward next and stuck her dagger in Naree's collarbone. Naree immediately burst into flames. Fire erupted everywhere around the room. Karina ducked her head, wrapping her arms around herself. She felt the water that had just drenched her evaporate from the heat.

The flames covering Naree died down, leaving her intact and unscathed, but still, she heaved out heavy, labored breaths. The changes must have been doing unspeakable things to her.

The next dark mage—Harish—came forward. His jaw was squared as he jammed his dagger into her side. Her scream echoed through the crypt, and Karina swore it shook the air. The burst of black smoke blew quickly away as Naree was bathed in a deep green glow. A ferocious wind tore through the place, sending debris flying. Karina had to squint as she struggled to stand in place and not get blown back.

The elite mages seemed to be frozen in place, still floating six inches from the ground. Their expressions spoke of sorrow and anger and defeat.

When the next dark mage approached Naree and drove his dagger into her, a forceful soundwave crescendoed through the room, shattering headstones and cracking statues. Naree's body was a glowing blue vibration, barely solid at all. Her scream left a ringing in Karina's ears, even as the blue glow disappeared.

The final dark mage stepped up to the sarcophagus and stabbed his dagger into Naree's shoulder. She threw her head back as a purple glow covered her body. It looked as though she were turning into smoke. And then the entire crypt filled with purple smoke.

Karina let out a barrage of coughs as she tried to see through the haze. Just when she thought she was going to choke to death, the smoke began to disappear, revealing Naree panting on the sarcophagus, covered in blood.

It was Bhutano's turn. He used two hands as he lifted his dagger and plunged in into the center of Naree's chest.

He barely let go of the hilt as a bright, white light blasting from Naree's body expanded, swallowing everything in its path in a blinding shimmer. Everything went white, and Karina was suddenly overcome with emotion. She sobbed in the lonely, white light.

Little by little, the intensity of the white light faded. As the details of the crypt became clearer, Karina found that the elite mages—as well as the dark mages and Bhutano—were crumpled on the floor. The stone lid of the sarcophagus had slid open, sitting askew. Naree was on her knees beside the stone coffin, her eyes bloodshot, her face pale, and her body drenched in sweat and blood.

Nineteen

Mayhara opened her eyes. Her cheek was pressed against the hard floor of the crypt. She flexed her fingers, shocked she was finally able to move. Her body was sore. It felt like she'd been run over by a truck. And no wonder; she and the other elite mages had been doused with torrential waves of water, blasted by fire, pummeled by an explosion of elemental magic, and there'd been no escaping it. Because she'd been frozen in place and rendered helpless by Naree's powers.

She slowly lifted her head. Jae groaned beside her. She reached out and curled a finger around one of his. He twisted so he could see her. She wanted to ask if he was all right, but she couldn't find her voice just yet.

"Oh, no."

It was Darshana's voice. She'd been protecting herself behind a tall headstone during Naree's transformations, and now she was creeping out into the open, staring, pale-faced, at the sarcophagus.

Mayhara reached deep down inside herself and found the strength to sit up. The sound of stone scraping against stone echoed throughout the crypt. A dark figure loomed beneath the light filtering in from the ceiling.

Two small slivers of silver stared out beneath a black, tattered hood. The figure moved slowly, deliberately. His form was enormous, bigger than any man Mayhara had ever seen. But when the light hit his face, she could see that his snake-like skin was sunken into his skull.

The dark mages gaped at him in awe. Bhutano was the first to present himself to his lord, kneeling before him and

DIAMOND *Mage*

bowing his head, his arms stretched forward and palms flat on the floor. The dark mages followed suit, falling in place beside Bhutano.

A howling wind stirred up the dust in the room as Kashmeru stepped out of his coffin. He looked down at Naree, who was still on the floor, covered with blood. She looked up at him with a combination of fear and wonder.

"It is time." His voice was deep and slow and full of power.

He extended a hand to Naree. There was a moment of hesitation before she took it and rose to her feet. There was no smile on her face as the tears began to flow.

"My love." Kashmeru pulled her into his arms. He traced her cheek with his hand and then leaned down to kiss her.

Naree let out a small moan, throwing her arms around him.

After the kiss ended, Kashmeru leaned back to look at her.

"Our destiny has arrived. And now it is time to be rid of this world and move on to our own." Kashmeru pushed back his hood, exposing his hairless head.

Mayhara could now see that the dark skin at his cheeks

167

were made up of scales.

Kashmeru closed his eyes. A swirling black mist rose up around him. He lifted his arms, taking Naree's hand with him.

Mayhara couldn't understand the words leaving his mouth, but she could feel them. It felt as if everything inside of her and everything around her was breaking apart, crumbling and rotting, becoming void of life.

"We have to do this now," Yuki said to Mayhara, suddenly at her side. "Before he destroys the world."

Mayhara turned to Jae. "The spell." She searched his face. "It might kill your sister."

Jae's eyes darted between Mayhara and Naree. He winced, also feeling the destruction inside of him as Kashmeru worked his magic. Biting down hard on his lip, he gave Mayhara a solemn nod.

Mayhara sucked in a shuddered breath and stood. Yuki hurried to her feet and held her hand. In unison, they recited the spell.

"Abire hostem
Hoc planum es ex agro
Cum enim venenum componere

> *boni a Chakras*
> *Abire hostem*
> *Vos ultra*
> *Per virtute divina*
> *demoliti sunt egressi vobiscum*
> *et non est amplius."*

She knew the spell would do nothing coming from them, but if Karina would hear them and recite the incantation herself, the spell could take effect.

Mayhara stared at Karina, hoping she would understand. Karina's jaw hung open as she listened. On their third run of the incantation, she joined in.

> *"Abire hostem*
> *Hoc planum es ex agro*
> *Cum enim venenum componere*
> *boni a Chakras*
> *Abire hostem*
> *Vos ultra*
> *Per virtute divina*
> *demoliti sunt egressi vobiscum*
> *et non est amplius."*

Mayhara thought it was another earthquake, but it was Kashmeru's low cry of anger.

With a jerk of his hand, a thick, black whip snapped in Mayhara's direction. She and Yuki were smacked back, flying through the air and slamming into stone statues.

Her vision blurred and her head throbbed from connecting with the stone. In a matter of seconds, Jae was at her side, pulling her into his arms.

She thought all was lost, but Karina was still chanting. Mayhara lifted her head. Kashmeru threw his dark magic at the witch, but she seemed to have some sort of bubble of protection around her. Nothing he did could get through. Her magic repelled his every move.

As she continued the incantation, a tiny burst of energy sparked near the ceiling. It was a bluish gaseous nebula that spread, stretching across the ceiling and getting thicker as it descended upon Kashmeru and Naree.

Harish stood and tried to syphon the cloud, but his magic didn't work. He and the other mages began coughing, grabbing at their necks. Ru stared wide-eyed at her skin as it began to blister and bubble up into black, crusty sores. Bhutano let out a cry as his skin turned to liquid and oozed off his body.

Naree held her throat, choking on the blue gas as she doubled over. "Poison," she whispered in a raspy voice.

Kashmeru gaped at the goddess, attempting to help her, but it wasn't working. "No," he cried. "No! My love!"

She reached for him, gasping for breath. Her lips, and then her face and her neck, began to turn blue. As she fell into his arms, he let out a gruff scream.

"Kash... me... ru..."

He shook his head. "No. Lakshmi. My love. You can't die!"

She placed a hand on his jaw, her lips parted as she struggled to breathe.

He leaned down and kissed her. Together, they fell to their knees. At first, Mayhara didn't understand, but then, as the kiss continued, the blue hue slowly drained from Naree's skin. As Kashmeru syphoned the poison from her body, his lips and jaw turned blue. When the last of the poison left her body, she fell limp and passed out. She slipped from his arms when his body began to stiffen. His throat glowed blue, and his eyes rolled back in his head. The blue skin spread, then turned to gray. The gray hardened, cracked, and crumbled into powder, bit by bit carried off by the wind until Kashmeru was no more.

#

Jae jumped up and ran to Naree's side. He cradled her head in his lap and searched for a pulse. Her silk gown was drenched in blood. The corpses of the dark mages surrounding them began suffering the same fate as Kashmeru, the dust from their bodies blowing away in the wind.

Karina had done it. She had destroyed Kashmeru. But at what cost?

Jae felt around Naree's neck, wishing his own heart would stop pounding long enough that he could feel his sister's pulse.

"Naree, please," he whispered.

The other mages joined him, all gathered around. They crouched down, their faces full of sadness.

"Is she—" Salina couldn't even continue.

Mayhara lay her head on Jae's shoulder and reached out to take Naree's hand.

Yuki's cheeks were stained with tears. She dropped to her knees and placed her hand on Naree's shoulder. Salina sobbed, taking Naree's other hand. Shiro and Loni placed their hands upon Naree's arm. Penny stroked Naree's forehead.

Darshana stood before them, Karina at her side, and intertwined her fingers, holding her hands against her chin.

Jae suddenly felt a warmth beneath his fingers. He searched Naree's form and spotted the glow beneath the hand of each elite mage. The stones on their wristbands shone, and the different-colored lights moved over the surface of Naree's body. The red light of the garnet moved to the position of the root chakra, the orange to the sacral chakra, and so on, until all seven lights were aligned.

The lights glowed brighter and then, all at once, disappeared. Naree's eyes opened as she let out a gasp.

Jae couldn't believe his eyes. Naree slowly sat up, looking around at the elite mages as if in disbelief. She brought her hands to her lips and shook her head. "After all I did to you, you still saved me." She sniffed back tears. "I'm so sorry. So truly sorry. I... I wasn't me. I couldn't control—"

Jae wiped a tear from her cheekbone. "Of course. We know."

He pulled her close for an embrace, not wanting to let her go.

"We're here to serve you," Shiro said.

Mayhara nodded. "You have your loyal army."

Naree sniffled back her tears. "And I'm ready to lead you. And to make it all up to you."

Jae hugged her again.

"Why didn't the poison affect us?" Salina suddenly asked, looking up at Darshana.

"I wouldn't let it," Karina said with a wink.

Darshana placed an arm around Karina and smiled.

"Sorry to interrupt."

They all looked up to see Qiang and Mitty standing near the entrance of the crypt.

"You might want to come upstairs," Qiang said. "We've rounded everyone up and are holding those responsible under citizen's arrest, in the name of the Empire of the Lotus. We just need our empress to instruct us what to do with them." He bowed. "Your Highness."

Naree's gaze went around to all the elite mages. With one curt nod, she stood, looking graceful and regal despite her blood-soaked dress. She lifted her chin, a determination setting in. "Yes. Let's get started."

Twenty

Mayhara adjusted the black sash of her uniform. The red, military-style jacket was crisp and clean, the silver buttons shining. The pearled lotus pin sat near her shoulder, reminding her of the trials and tribulations she'd gone through to get to where she was now.

"Mayhara?"

She turned to find Yuki standing at the door. Her jacket—the same as Mayhara's but in white—was a stark contrast to her decorated black sash.

"Your family has arrived," Yuki said with a smile.

Mayhara ran her fingers over the braided bun of her dark hair and followed Yuki into the hall.

She was in a part of the palace that held the commanders' apartments. As elites, the mages were assigned quarters to live in, but the empress made it clear that they were free to have residences elsewhere if they pleased, as long as it didn't interfere with their duties. She made it clear that she wanted to remain fair and just in all her rulings.

The commanders' quarters—along with the empress's chambers and the throne room—had been the first of the palace to be restored. Construction would soon begin to restore the academy.

Mayhara walked swiftly down the sunlit hall to the red-carpeted stairs. She had seen her family the very day the prison camps had been abolished, but for all the years she'd been away from them, one reunion was never enough.

Yuki gave her a wink as she disappeared down the hall.

"Mama, Papa!" Mayhara found them outside the throne room, embracing them immediately. Her parents looked older, their hair grayed, and wrinkles worn into their skin. She turned to her sisters—younger spitting images of herself— and placed kisses upon their cheeks.

"Are they really going to rebuild the academy?" her youngest sister, Anjana, asked.

"Yes, and you and Kakoli will both be students. You'll be taught by the finest guru in New United Asia. And I'll be there too, just in case you get into any trouble."

"As a teacher?" Kakoli asked, she and Anjana both seemingly please with the prospect of attending the academy.

"That too. But I have a sworn duty to serve and protect the empress as well." Mayhara smiled, reveling in the fact that she shared this duty with Jae, and that they would be together always.

"We are so thrilled to have been invited to the coronation," Mayhara's mother said, smoothing out her crimson sari.

"Of course." Mayhara placed a hand on her elbow. "It's the least the empire can do for you for the terrible years you suffered. Come. Let's go inside and find your seats."

The throne room's marble floors practically sparkled in the sunlight that streamed in through the floor-to-ceiling gilded windows. The room was filled with chairs—most of them already occupied—facing a dais, upon which sat a magnificent throne.

Mayhara brought her family to their seats. "I have to finish preparing for the ceremony. But I'll see you afterward."

She left the room through the back, which connected to an adjoining preparation room. Karina stood outside the door, waiting for the ceremony to begin, and gave Mayhara a wave. As Mayhara entered the adjoining room, she ran into Shiro, almost knocking him over.

"Sorry," he told her.

She laughed. "No, it's my fault. Wait. I messed up your sash. Let me fix it."

She straightened his sash and brushed lint from his copper jacket. "Is Qiang coming?"

"You mean General Tsai?" He winked.

"Yes, of course."

Shiro smiled. "You know he wanted to be named a

knight instead?" He laughed and shook his head. "Yes, I do believe the empress expects his presence."

"And will he stay for the party after?"

"I do believe that *I* expect his presence, yes."

They laughed together just as Loni entered the room. She narrowed her eyes at them.

"You talking about me?" she asked. She checked her emerald green jacket. "Did I button it wrong or something?"

Shiro raised a brow, and Mayhara bit the inside of her cheek.

"No," Mayhara said. "You look great."

Even though Loni walked past her with eyes still narrowed, Mayhara knew it was just for show. They had actually had a nice talk after the showdown with Kashmeru. Mayhara had told Loni about seeing Kanya in the spirit realm and delivered the hug Kanya had asked her to give Loni. That hug had changed things between them, and Mayhara was looking forward to building a friendship with her.

Yuki walked into the room with Penny, who looked amazing in her purple jacket and black sash.

"Hey," Penny called. "It's almost time. Has anyone

seen Salina?"

"She's out front," Loni said. "Vano just got here."

"Is Patrin here too?" Shiro asked.

"Yeah," Loni answered. "He's catching up with Mr. Kitaro. Probably sulking in secret because he lost Darshana to him."

"Ooh," Yuki joked. "Love triangle."

"Yeah." Loni smirked. "Those are the worst."

The doors to the garden opened, and Jae stood in the doorway, fixing the lapels of his sapphire blue jacket. He caught Mayhara's eye and she closed the distance between them.

"Hey." Mayhara looked past Jae. "How is she?"

Sitting on the steps to the garden, Naree stared off into the distance. She looked so regal in her silver gown, hair swept up and waiting for her crown.

Naree would get this way sometimes, Mayhara discovered. When it counted, she filled the role of empress with diligence and competence. But when there weren't too many eyes on her, she would withdraw, sitting alone and staring off, as if she were waiting for something. As if she were missing someone.

Jae had said he thought she would need some time.

She was heartbroken. She'd lost a love she'd had since the beginning of time. He believed she knew that the relationship had been toxic, but still, that didn't mean her soul was any less crushed.

"She's okay," Jae said. "She'll be in in a minute."

"She's the empress." Mayhara shrugged one shoulder. "She can take all the time she needs."

"In that case," Jae said, taking her hands in his, "that means I have time to do this."

He leaned closer, his gaze on her lips. She couldn't help but smile as she tipped her head up to accept his kiss.

"You promise me a dance later?" she asked when the kiss ended.

"Do I have to?"

She cupped his cheek. "You do," she joked. "I'm afraid it's simply a fate you can't escape."

In case you missed them...

Be sure to check out first six books in the

Empire of the Lotus series:

Available in print and ebook from all online retailers

CRIMSON MAGE

http://books2read.com/crimsonmage

COPPER MAGE

http://books2read.com/coppermage

GOLDEN MAGE

http://books2read.com/goldenmage

EMERALD MAGE

http://books2read.com/emeraldmage

SAPPHIRE MAGE

http://books2read.com/sapphiremage

AMETHYST MAGE

http://books2read.com/amethystmage

ACKNOWLEDGEMENTS

It's a little sad to say goodbye to this series. I feel so connected to it and its characters. Like old friends. But it's been a blast, and I'm so glad I was able to share the story with the world. I hope it touched a few hearts.

As always, I thank my family, my friends, my colleagues, my Snowy Wings family, and my agent—Italia Gandolfo—for their continuous support and encouragement. A special shoutout to my ARC team, a brilliant collection of readers who swallow up my stories like candy: Kalli Bunch, Darcy Smith, Christine Gribble, Tina Merrit. Kimberly Grube, Athena Lee Brown, Melinda Goosen, Whitney Godard, Debbie Eyre, Becky Brown, Teri Ruscak, Heather Bane, and the rest of the amazing team—thank you so so much for indulging in my story!

Please, my dear readers, stay tuned for more. I have another series coming to fruition soon.

ABOUT THE AUTHOR

Dorothy Dreyer is a Philippine-born American living in Germany with her husband, her two college kids, and two Siberian Huskies. She is an award-winning, *USA Today* Bestselling Author of young adult and new adult books that usually have some element of magic or the supernatural in them. Aside from reading, she enjoys movies, binge-watching series, chocolate, take-out, traveling, and having fun with friends and family.

You can find out more about Dorothy on her website: http://dorothydreyer.com

Like YA Fantasy?

Check out the award-winning CURSE OF THE

PHOENIX duology:

PHOENIX DESCENDING

http://books2read.com/phoenixdescending

Solo Medalist winner of the 2018 New Apple

Summer eBook awards in the category

Young Adult Fantasy

Who must she become in order to survive?

Since the outbreak of the phoenix fever in Drothidia, Tori Kagari has already lost one family member to the fatal disease. Now, with the fever threatening to wipe out her entire family, she must go against everything she believes in order to save them—even if that means making a deal with the enemy.

When Tori agrees to join forces with the unscrupulous Khadulians, she must take on a false identity in order to infiltrate the queendom of Avarell and fulfill her part of the bargain, all while under the watchful eye of the unforgiving Queen's Guard. But time is running out, and every lie, theft, and abduction she is forced to carry out may not be enough to free her family or herself from death.

And …

PARAGON RISING

http://books2read.com/paragonrising

Book Two

in the

Curse of the Phoenix duology

On the brink of war, the fate of the nine realms lies in Tori Kagari's hands. After her arduous efforts to infiltrate the queendom of Avarell, Tori must now escape from it in an unforeseen alliance with a runaway princess and the soldier who saved Tori's life.

When the savage forces of Nostidour take hold of Avarell, Tori must seek out the rulers of the other realms and convince them to join the fight. But when the other realms discover that Tori has been lying about who she is, they are hesitant to trust her. Now Tori must find a way to prove herself, even if it means leading the battle herself and risking everything in the name of peace.

Also from Snowy Wings Publishing

WHEN DARKNESS WHISPERS

by Heather L. Reid

https://www.snowywingspublishing.com/book/when-darkness-whispers/

It's time to choose: Love or lies, faith or fear, darkness or destiny.

Quinn Taylor hasn't slept through the night in months. Not since the demons from her dreams began materializing in the school hallway, feeding on her fears, and whispering of her death. Trading in her cheerleading uniform for caffeine drinks to keep the nightmares at bay, Quinn's life is in ruins from the demons' torment until Aaron, an amnesiac with a psychic ability, accidentally enters her dreams. He's the light in her darkness and she's the key to his past, but the last thing the demons want is for them to be together.

To keep them apart, the demons must convince Quinn that Aaron will betray her or, worse, confirm her fear that she's crazy. Aaron and Quinn's combined powers could banish the darkness for good, but only if she learns to trust her heart and he recovers the secret locked away in his fragile memory. That is, unless the demons kill them first.

ALL THE TALES WE TELL

by Annie Cosby

https://books2read.com/u/3nvO6P

She's filthy rich. He's not. It'll take patience, an old woman who thinks she's a selkie, and one salty-sweet summer on the beach to make them realize what's between them.

When Cora's mother whisks the family away for the summer, Cora must decide between forging her future in the glimmering world of second homes where her parents belong, or getting lost in the enchanting world of the locals and the mystery surrounding a lonely old woman who claims to be a selkie—and who probably needs Cora more than anyone else.

Through the fantastical tales and anguished memories of the batty Mrs. O'Leary, as well as the company of a particularly gorgeous local boy called Ronan, Cora finds an escape from the reality of planning her life after high school. But will it come at the cost of alienating Cora's mother, who struggles with her own tragic memories?

As the summer wanes, it becomes apparent that Mrs. O'Leary is desperate to leave Oyster Beach. And Ronan just may hold the answer to her tragic past—and Cora's future.

FANGS AND FINS

by Amy McNulty

https://books2read.com/b/boYLaL

A sleepy town hiding an ancient war. Two teenagers stuck in the middle. Will graduation be a permanent end?

Bookworm Ember Goodwin was looking for romance her senior year, not a new, popular-girl stepsister. And things get heated when a mesmerizing stranger in sunglasses vies for their attention. But when Ember wakes with a thirst for blood, she discovers her dreamy beau is hiding a supernatural-sized secret that could leave her sleeping in a coffin.

Queen bee Ivy Sheppard wishes her dad hadn't moved them in with his new wife just in time for her final year of high school. But when a budding romance with an aquatically gifted hunk leaves her with icy abilities, her unstable world turns upside down. Because an ancient feud is about to pit her against her nerdy stepsister in a fierce fight to the death.

Swept off her feet and growing in power, Ember will do anything for her undead boyfriend. But Ivy vows to put a stop to the paranormal mayhem before their newly blended family loses a daughter.

Will the two young women forge peace between warring magical worlds… or die for the ones they love?

AQUA

by Tracy Korn

https://books2read.com/u/b62XVM

Hold your breath…

The future is three miles underwater, and Jazwyn Ripley's time has come.

Earth's atmosphere will only support a few more generations, and most of advanced society has already relocated to the sea. To survive, only one option remains for the Topsiders—get into Gaia Sur, the elite academy on the ocean floor.

But after Jazwyn Ripley trains a lifetime for the chance, something is wrong in the interviews. Her evaluation isn't like those of her soul-rattled classmates, and now, Arco Hart is desperate to protect her from something he won't talk about.

Cryptic messages coming from the earth's core. A charming, but infamous rival who knows why.

Everything is telling her to walk away, but for the

struggling class at the bottom, there's nowhere to go but down.

The road to everything the cadets ever wanted turns out to lead somewhere they never intended to go, and one decision will change the course of their lives for good:

Continue on the scripted path, or chase something deeper?

Find these books and more at

https://www.snowywingspublishing.com/books

Made in United States
Orlando, FL
17 March 2024

44864576R00133